JOURNEY INTO DARKNESS

a story in four parts

part 1

On the Eve of Conflict

part 2

Up From Corinth

part 3

Across the Valley to Darkness

part 4

Toward the End of the Search

ON THE EVE OF CONFLICT

the beginning of the story
JOURNEY INTO DARKNESS

written by
J. Arthur Moore

Author's Note:

Journey Into Darkness was begun some years ago. It is finally being written at the request of Charley French, one of several campers who heard the story while on camping trips with the author. Learning the original story had not been worked on for some time, he offered to represent the main character if the author would continue to work on the story. So for him and others who have enjoyed the telling of *Journey Into Darkness* this book is written.

Another camper, Michael Flanagan, suggested the format of the story. On behalf of the many young readers who do not like thick books, he felt several smaller books would be more appropriate. Therefore the story of *Journey Into Darkness* is told in a series of four books.

All photography is by the author. Duane Kinkade is represented by Charlie French and Jaimie Fowler is represented by Richie Christman. All youngsters are participants in camping programs directed by the author.

Copyright © 2013 by J. Arthur Moore

Library of Congress Control Number:		2013905483
ISBN:	Hardcover	978-1-4836-1589-9
	Softcover	978-1-4836-1588-2
	Ebook	978-1-4836-1590-5

This is a work of historic fiction. An intricate blend of fact and fiction, the thread of experience of the fictitious boy soldier runs through the fabric of a very real war and its historic violence exactly as it happened.

This book was printed in the United States of America.

Rev. date: 03/27/2013

To order additional copies of this book, contact:
Xlibris Corporation
1-888-795-4274
www.Xlibris.com
Orders@Xlibris.com
133371

Dedication

On the Eve of Conflict is dedicated in His love to Charley French and Richie Christman, each of whom has helped by becoming forever a part of the story through the photographic material, and to all who have enjoyed its telling and shared in the adventure of its creation.

Duane Kinkade

Jamie Fowler

The head of the ax hung momentarily suspended in the air before it was drawn forcefully downward. As it struck the chunk of tree round with a loud crack, the grain collapsed and the cord wood flew apart. The ax blade bit into the chopping stump and there it stayed. The man paused to wipe the sweat from his eyebrows with the back of his hand, while the boy bent to gather up the pieces of wood from where they had fallen about the wood yard.

Andrew Kinkade was a man of enthusiastic energy. Nearing his thirty-fourth birthday, he was small in stature with unexpected strength from years of work on the farm and, in earlier years, at the store the family once owned. He picked up his plain, light-colored shirt from where it lay across the rough, wooden saw horse and wiped the wood chips from his arms and head before shaking the shirt out and slipping it on. He watched his son stack the last of the wood while he tucked in his shirt tail and pulled on his suspender straps.

"Son, what ya say we call this done fer now 'n head off fishin fer a bit?" The man paused with his thumbs hooked in the waistband of his trousers.

Duane tossed the last of the pieces onto the stack of split wood. "Sure, Pa," the boy responded. "I'm ready fer it. My feet'll like ta hang in the water 'n cool off." He parked himself on the stack of wood to catch his breath. "Hey, Pounder!" he called.

The large tan and white head of his long-haired mixed-breed dog raised itself from behind the scattering of unsplit rounds beyond the chopping block. The large mouth opened wide in a lazy yawn, then he shook his head to dislodge a bothersome fly. Dark eyes met dark eyes as the dog awaited his young master's expected command.

"Com 'ere, boy." The boy slapped his thigh lightly. "Ya wanna go fishin?"

Slowly the dog stretched, then pushed himself to his feet. Shuffling around the scattered wood chunks, he worked his way to where the boy waited and sank into a seated position by his side, resting his muzzle in the boy's lap. The ten-year-old boy gently stroked his friend's neck and scratched him under the ears. Duane was of slight build and somewhat short in stature. Pounder, while still a pup, not yet a year old, stood fully as tall as the boy and outweighed him by an extra ten pounds. They were the best of friends, inseparable from the day they met in a back alley of the nearby town of Bendton. Lifting his head, Pounder reached out to lick the side of the boy's face, in complete agreement with the fishing idea. The pass of the large tongue from under the chin, up the cheek, and across the ear, tickled; and Duane drew back, jumping to his feet.

Mr. Kinkade spoke, "Why don't you two find us some worms whilst I see 'bout gittin the poles from the barn."

"Okay," the boy called, already on his way toward the tree-shaded end of the garden. "Meet ya at the rocks near the lane ta the creek."

Pounder followed as the two ran off to search the garden's edge and nearby rocks. Duane's bare feet padded across the yard, sending up small clouds of dust. Sweat streaked the boy's tanned flesh, staining the waistband of his trousers and darkening the edges of his suspender straps. Dust quickly attached itself in a thin coating to the moisture of his skin from the waist up.

The dog ran ahead and began to pick at the small rocks, digging gingerly with his paws. As Duane joined him, he rolled one over, then sat to watch the boy inspect for worms. A quick grab captured one single creature as it began to burrow into the dirt. The search continued. Pounder turned over the stones, then dug into the soft soil of the garden while Duane caught what few worms could be uncovered. A short time later Mr. Kinkade approached with poles and an old coffee tin which they used for carrying bait.

"Got eny?" the man asked.

"Seven," his son replied.

"Thet'll do." The boy stood to share his prizes. "Here." His father held out the can and the worms were safely deposited. A handful of dirt was added and the nail-punched lid was secured.

Pounder observed that preparations were complete, so he started ahead to tend to the serious business of hunting rabbits along the way. As the dog raced off ahead, the man handed his son his pole and they turned to follow. The pole was a green willow branch with a length of string from the general store and a regular store-bought hook. The dog's excited bark signalled a chase was on. Duane smiled to himself, for he knew the rabbit would win in the end.

The boy and his father followed the worn lane between the garden and the corn field until it passed around a small knoll and into a stand of pine trees. They took their time and ambled slowly along. The boy paused to watch a squirrel bound across the pine needles and disappear into a tree. The man stopped to witness the wonder his son had for creatures. They moved on, the boy taking the lead.

"Pa," Duane spoke without turning. "Ya think ther's gonna be a war?"

"I dunno, Son." They both continued to walk on. "Ther's a lot a talk. I really think there might."

Nothing more was said for several minutes. Sunlight shown in a bright splotch ahead where the woodland gave way to an open meadow.

"Ya gonna go if there is?" the boy asked.

"I hafta do what's right by you 'n yer ma 'n by this land. So I s'pose so."

The sudden brightness enveloped the two as they entered the meadow. Shading their eyes against the glare, they paused a moment to get used to the light, then moved on. The land sloped in a gentle down-hill roll, until it bottomed out at a broad meandering creek which coursed its way across the heart of the grassland. The spring grass was knee-high with splashes of color from wild flowers and the deep purple of thistles in bloom. As the man and the boy approached the water's edge, the dog came splashing through the shallows along the shore to join them. Bounding up the embankment, he paused to shake the water from his long coat and for a brief moment was lost in a mist that sparkled in a fine dusty glitter of sunlight. The three then headed down-stream to a deep pool of quiet water shaded by a large, knarled oak tree. There they settled down for the serious business of fishing.

Mr. Kinkade found his regular place at the base of the tree where he sat with his back against its trunk. Once comfortable, he began to bait his hook and drop it in. Duane nestled into a favorite position among the rocks along the bank. Pounder lay on the grass nearby, head on front paws, where he could quietly survey the boy's progress, keep a watchful eye on their surroundings, and doze when he felt bored.

An uneventful hour slipped by. Nothing much was said. The fish weren't biting. It was a time of quiet peace. Small sparrows chirped and flitted about in the grass along the creek's bank. A black water snake slithered along the water's surface to crawl out on a large rock near the far bank and sun itself in the warmth of the afternoon. Dragon flies hovered above the water near the tall grass in the shallows. Water spiders danced in interlacing rings on its surface. Duane left his pole propped in the rocks and concentrated on a search among the stones for salamanders and crawfish. His father slipped into a quiet nap, dozing where he sat. Pounder lay motionless except for his eyes. They followed every move the boy made.

Suddenly there was a loud splash as Mr. Kinkade's line came to life and the pole was dragged into the water. Andrew awoke with a start, in time to see the dog spring to his feet and leap into the water after the fishing pole. Duane turned to see what the sudden commotion was about and saw his father standing on the creek bank, watching Pounder chase after the fishing pole.

Snatching the base of the pole, the dog struggled with his prize, working his way backwards toward the embankment. A large catfish splashed about on the end of the line, fighting against being pulled ashore. The man leaned down to take the incoming pole as his son hurried closer to be part of the excitement. The pole came within reach when the fish made a sudden dive beside a large underwater rock. The line snagged. Andrew took the pole and pulled while the dog scrambled up the bank to stand by the boy and supervise. Suddenly the line snapped and the contest was ended.

"Almost, Pa," Duane commented.

Pounder took time to shake off the water and the boy hurried backwards, raising his hand to shield himself from the spray.

His father smiled at the sight. "Guess fishin's done fer now," he observed. Glancing skyward, he continued, "Git'n on t'wards supper. Time ta be headin in."

"Soon's I fetch m' pole 'n the bait can." Duane retrieved the things from their place along the bank, then joined his father.

As before, the dog ran ahead. The boy and his father followed. Laughing together about the story they would tell his ma about the one that got away, they headed toward the wooded path and disappeared into the shadows.

*   *   *

As the first rays of sunlight raced out of the east, the early morning mists were scattered, revealing the glistening trees and the freshly plowed fertile fields along either side of the river valley. Nestled along the south bank of the river was the bustling little village of Bendton, with the glow of the morning sun glinting off the belfry of its little church. About five miles up river, and set over a mile back from the water in a small glen on the hillside, was the little farm, full of the early morning sounds and sights generated by the coming of a new spring day.

Whiffs of smoke rising from the cabin's chimney suggested that breakfast was being prepared. The wood-frame cabin was small. It had only three rooms—a main one for dining and living and two tiny bedrooms. The yard was scattered with cackling hens, and from a fencepost somewhere in the barnyard a rooster raised its morning call. From the barn came the sounds of a lowing cow, a horse's whinny, and the clatter of a pail. The morning chores were underway.

The barn, like the house, was of wood construction and small in size. It contained but a few tools and some livestock. The hay was stacked in a grain yard beside the structure. A small flat-bed wagon was kept outside the board fence that surrounded the barn yard. The old wood-plank gate sagged from use and age. Missing shingles from the roof showed dark holes near the ridge of the steep slope.

Laura Kinkade, a small, slip of a woman in her thirties, with her dark hair pinned up in a bun on the back of her head, emerged from the cabin wearing a dark plain dress and an apron. She called toward the barn, "Dee! you git yerself an yer pa in here an warshed up fer brekfist fer it gits cold! An mind ya use both hands when ya bring the milk this time! I want 'nough in the dipper ta bottle taday."

"Yea, Ma," replied the boy indifferently, as he stepped from the barn into the early morning brightness.

He paused briefly, squinting his eyes against the glare. His pa joined him a moment later and the two stood at the barn door for a minute. Pounder lay along the wall beside the open door. He stood as the two emerged and padded silently to the boy's side.

"Ya take the milk ta yer Ma, Dee, 'n mind what she says 'bout usin two hands. I'll turn the calf in with her ma 'n be right along."

"Sure, Pa," affirmed the boy as he started for the house.

The dog kept pace alongside as the boy crossed the yard to the house. Duane set the milk on the porch while he went around to the side of the house where the pump and water trough were. Pounder stopped at the corner of the structure to watch while the boy washed his hands and face in the trough. Then with eyes shut tight against the water dripping from his hair, Duane reached blindly for the towel that hung on the pump handle. The dog sat down to wait. Duane's father arrived from the barn just in time to catch the towel as the back of the boy's hand brushed against it, sending it sliding from the pump handle toward the ground.

"If you'd only larn ta open yer eyes, I wouldn't haf ta play at rescuer like this." He smiled as he handed Duane the towel.

The boy dried his face and hands, and flicked the towel across the top of the pump. Pushing his brown hair back out of his eyes, he headed back toward the porch where he picked up the milk, mounted the steps, and entered the main room. The dog followed as far as the steps. There he plopped down with a thud to nap while the family ate.

The tantalizing smell of hot cakes filled the room. Duane placed the milk on the table and went over to the stove to watch the bubbles pop as the batter grew and burst on the griddle.

"If'n ya don't set yerself down ta the table, yer not gonna git nothin ta eat." The words came with a smile as the boy's mother flipped the cakes and he went to his seat.

"Call yer Pa, Dee," Mrs. Kinkade instructed without turning from the stove.

"No need ta, Son," her husband remarked as he entered the cabin and hung his coat on its peg beside the door. "Smelled them hotcakes clear outside 'n figured I'd best hurry if'n I was ta git some 'fer Dee ate 'em all."

They sat down to breakfast and the man said grace. Then as they ate, he discussed the plans for the day.

"Dee," his father instructed, "I want ya ta fill the woodbox fer yer Ma 'n have a bucket a water in here fer her. I've ta go ta town ta git what groc'ries 'n supplies I kin, 'n I figure ya kin be a help. So soon's brekfist is don, ya git ta be doin them chores so's ta be ready when I am."

"You bet, Pa!" exclaimed the boy.

The thought of going to town excited Duane so that he forgot to open his mouth as he attempted to take in a forkful of hotcake dripping with molasses. He quickly looked to see if his Pa had noticed. After all a grown boy of ten doesn't usually miss his mouth when it comes to getting in food. He knew his Ma hadn't noticed, cause she would have said something immediately.

"Is there enythin I kin git ya while I'm ta town, Laura?" the man asked his wife.

"I'll give ya a list a what I need. Git what's there."

When he was finished with breakfast, Mr. Kinkade pushed his plate back, stretched his arms at his side, and settled back in his chair, folding them across his chest. He stared thoughtfully at the ceiling for a moment, then turned toward his son who was wiping up his plate with a last bit of hotcake.

"On my way, Pa," Duane said as he gulped it down and hurriedly scraped his chair back from the table.

The boy skipped out the door to do as he had been instructed, grabbing the water bucket en route as he passed the drain board.

"Come on, Pounder," he called as he went. "We're goin ta town taday."

The dog jumped up to follow.

Mr. Kinkade followed along a short time later to hitch the team to the wagon. Within the quarter hour they were up in the wagon seat and ready to roll. The dog centered himself in the wagon bed, just behind the seat where he could peer ahead between the man and his son or survey the countryside as it rolled past.

"When shall I 'spect ya back?" Mrs. Kinkade asked.

"We ought ta be back sometime late aftanoon," her husband replied.

"Take good care a yerselfs, now. 'N don't go findin no trouble," she called after them as they left the farm yard and headed for the road. It wasn't that she expected them to get into trouble. It was just something more to say before they were gone, leaving her no one to talk to until they returned.

The sun was all the way up, now, and shining clear in the bright blue morning sky. As the horses ambled along, Duane couldn't help but to notice how sweet the air smelled and how carefree and unconcerned the jackrabbit feeding along the roadside seemed to be. The boy turned to observe the dog tense at the sight of the animal and reached out to calm him with a gentle stroking of the massive head. Then, resting his hand on the soft coat of the dog's back, he wondered what it would be like if there were to be a war as he had heard there might. There had been talk for a long time of secession, yet that hadn't happened. There might be a lot of excitement. But for now, war was just talk. He gazed into his friend's brown eyes, smiled, then went back to scanning the countryside.

An hour passed as the wagon rumbled the country roads, rolling up its small cloud of dust which caught in the morning breeze and drifted into nothing.

They approached the village of Bendton. The outskirts consisted of small farms with their frame buildings along the road and the fields stretching away on either side. Then they passed small clapboard homes, each on an acre or so of ground. Some had barns out back for a horse and a cow and maybe a few chickens, and some didn't. But all had little narrow shanties, each with its halo or aroma. In the center of the town were the hotel and saloons with their squared, weathered wood fronts, the shops, a bank, and down along the river, the warehouses and docks. Most structures were of wood construction. Some were stone or a clay brick.

But something wasn't right. Almost everyone in the little town was at the newspaper office. Mr. Kinkade halted the rig in front of the shop to hear what was going on and why all the excitement.

"So they fin'ly done it," commented one of the men.

"But are ya sure it's true?" asked a second.

"Here's proof in black 'n white. See fer yerself," replied the first.

"I didn't think they had 'tin 'em," observed a third.

"Will some'n please tell me what's up?" Duane's pa inquired. Some turned to notice him.

"Ain't ya heard, Andy? Abe Lincoln's done declared war!" was the answer. "Some a our men fired at a Fort Sumpter off East som'eres 'n Lincoln got mad."

Laughter rippled through the crowd. Pounder joined in with a sharp bark.

"Dee, ya best go look up Jamie. I've some un'spected business here ta tend ta," ordered the boy's father.

"But, Pa . . ."

"No but's 'bout it. Now take off."

The boy climbed down from the wagon as his dog jumped from the side to follow. Mr. Kinkade watched his son start down the street, kicking at the dirt and small stones to vent his anger, while his dog accompanied him quietly at his side. A worried sadness showed in a half smile. Duane walked toward the brick building near the center of town. It was the Marshall's office. His friend, Jamie, was Marshall Jonathan Fowler's son.

"Doggone it," Duane muttered to himself as he approached the office structure, "Why is't thet I always have ta be treated like a kid. Why can't I listen ta growd-up talk sometimes." He paused at the porch steps outside.

Pounder stopped and, with a soft whine of inquiry, looked up at his young master.

"It's okay, boy. Ya stay outside on the porch." He pointed to the shadowed wall near the door.

The dog bounded up to the wooden walk, crossed to his regular spot, then dropped quietly. Resting his muzzle on his forepaws, he followed the boy with his eyes, as he climbed the steps and entered the office.

"Hey, Jamie!" he greeted, "are we really at war now?"

But the office seemed empty. Then a headful of curly, black hair popped up from behind the marshall's desk and large brown eyes peered at him across the paper-littered writing surface. "Hi, Dee," the cheerful voice greeted.

"What ya doin?" Duane paused for his eyes to adjust to the dim interior light.

"Dropped some papers," the boy explained as he stood up, then perched himself on the corner of the desk top. "War?" he continued. "So I hear." He shuffled through the papers as Duane crossed the room and dropped himself into the marshall's wooden, swivel chair. "They need all the men they kin git. Nigh onta ever'one in town who thinks he kin fight has already signed up. Pa says he's gonna stay back ta defend 'gainst raiders. They seem ta be hittin closer, now."

"Raiders?" Duane was whirling himself around in circles. Snagging the desk with his toe, he halted his movement. Then leaning back, he propped his boots on the desktop to listen.

"Yea, groups a outlaws has bin raidin 'n burnin farms 'n small towns ta the north. Pa says they git closer ev'ry week." Jamie laid the papers in the middle of the desk as he hopped down and walked over toward a bookcase by the wall.

"I hope he's wrong." Duane spun the chair to follow his friend's movement. "Hey, when da the recruits leave?"

"They're s'posed ta head east on the riverboat out a Ozark come the end a the month," came Jamie's reply. He reached beside the case for a broom.

"How long ya think the war'll last?" Duane pushed the chair back, rocking on its spring.

"Most people say it'll be over in six weeks." Jamie leaned on the broom. "But I think they're wrong. Say, is yer Pa gonna sign up?"

"I dunno." The chair flopped forward. "I guess so."

"Hey, gimme a hand here." Jamie suddenly realized he wasn't getting any work done. "You straighten up the papers on Pa's desk whilst I finish sweeping the floor."

"Yea, okay." The boy spun the chair to face the desk, and the two of them set to work straightening up the office. Jamie swept the floor, directing the dirt under the cabinet in the corner. Duane divided the papers on the desk into two neat piles, one with pictures and the other without.

*   *   *

It was the edge of evening when the wagon turned off the road and onto the lane into the farm. The western sky was a brilliant flame color while a silver disk with a broken edge shown in the black-blue eastern sky. The cabin with its yellow squares of light was an inviting sight. The boy and his father, hungry from the trip, would soon sit down to supper.

*   *   *

The fire leapt merrily on the hearth. The supper dishes had been washed and put away, and the evening chores were done. Mr. Kinkade was sitting in his favorite chair and staring into the fire. His wife rocked slowly in her high-backed, wooden rocker, quietly darning socks for her husband. Duane lay on the rug in front of the hearth, drawing pictures on wrapping paper with pieces of charcoal. Pounder lay napping, close to his side.

The man did not take his eyes off the fire as he addressed his wife. "Laura." He paused. "Ya know the South is secedin ta become the Confederacy. Well I heard taday thet fightin broke out in South Carolina 'n Lincoln declared war." He stopped and turned toward her. "I signed up taday ta help defend Arkansas if she should come ta be attacked."

The boy dropped his piece of charcoal and looked up at his father. Even though he had expected his pa to sign up, the reality that he had actually done so came as a shock to him. His mother stood up and, laying her darning aside, walked over to where her husband sat. Tears welled up in her eyes and dampened her cheeks. He reached up and clasped her hands in his, then pulled her into his lap. The dog merely opened his eyes to watch, though sensed the boy was upset and tensed to move if the boy should.

"Oh, Andy!" she cried and buried her face in his arms. He stroked her hair gently as he held her close and tried hard not to cry.

Duane felt a sudden emptiness in the pit of his stomach. He left his drawings and slipped out to the porch. His cheeks glistened wet as he looked out toward the shadow that was the barn and up toward the broken moon. His mouth quivered and he began to shake all over. The dog slipped silently to his side where he sat and watched the troubled face of the boy he loved. Grasping a post at the edge of the porch, Duane held tightly as he stood sobbing silently, the tears streaking his face. Suddenly the boy ran from the porch toward the haystack beside the barn. He threw himself down, buried his face in his arms, and cried out his heartache to the hay. He lay there a long time asking God why there had to be a war and why his father had to go. Pounder followed to lay by his side and lick the tears from his face. Duane caressed the soft head, then wrapped his arm around the thickly coated neck in an affectionate embrace and buried his face in its softness. The tears flowed as Pounder whined his concern for his grieving master. Finally the boy calmed down enough to notice that someone was approaching.

"Dee?" his father spoke gently.

Duane rolled over onto his back and gazed at his pa. Mr. Kinkade sat down beside him and the boy crawled closer to his father and lay his head in the security of his pa's lap. For a few minutes neither spoke.

"Pa," the boy began, "why do ya have ta go? Can't they fight without ya?"

"Son, if ev'ry father thought they could fight without him, the South wouldn't stand a chance." He held his son affectionately, caressing his shoulders as he hugged him close.

They sat there quietly as the sky slowly rotated over their heads. Strong arms wrapped the boy gently and held him close, hoping to God that he would be coming back after the war. Duane looked at his father and saw the hurt and the worry that he was feeling as he gazed intently at his home. The man's eyes turned to his son.

"Ain't it time ya git ta bed? Yer ma'll wonder where ya got ta."

"Ain't tired, Pa. I couldn't sleep now nohow."

His father stood up bringing Duane to his feet by his shoulders. The dog rose to his feet and watched. Grasping the boy's right shoulder firmly, the man turned his son in the direction of the lane. Pounder eased himself to a seated position and watched them go. They strolled slowly down the dirt and gravel pathway and across the meadows to their favorite fishing hole. Dark silhouettes of trees against the starlit sky seemed to float overhead as they passed along the ground between them.

Ma watched them from the doorway as they drifted through the moonlight, growing smaller in the distance. She understood, and turned to the hearth to keep the fire going and to await their return. Pounder, too, understood. He returned to the house where he lay down at the top of the steps to await their return.

The glistening silvery meadow smelled sweet in the night air as father and son walked quietly side by side.

"Pa, what's war like?"

"I dunno, Son. I've neve been in one b'fore. I s'pose it's bloody 'n tirin 'n prob'ly som'thin cruel. I fig'r when men go ta war, they fergit the enemy is people jest like them."

They continued on quietly for a time. Passing through the stand of silent pines, they came upon the meadow. They went on until they reached the darkened shape that was the oak, and there they stopped. The water rippled and gurgled along, interrupted every once in a while by a flash and a splash as a catfish broke across the surface.

Duane watched in silence as he relaxed against the sturdy figure who stood behind him. His pa absentmindedly rubbed his son's arms against the chill night air.

"When the war's over, Dee, we'll come down here afta the big one out there. Next time he won't steal my pole."

They both smiled at the memory.

The two stood there a long time, like statues in the night. It was a special feeling, a need each had to be close to the other, knowing full well there was much to do before the parting, and there was a distinct possibility they would never see each other once his father left. An owl hooted in the distance. Crickets sang in the grass. The need passed. The two turned and started back toward the house.

The dog stood as his master and the man crossed the yard toward the house, then preceded them inside. Mrs. Kinkade was darning socks when they arrived, and laid her work aside as the two entered the cabin.

"Night, Pa," Dee whispered after they had closed the door for the night. He went to his ma and kissed her lightly on the cheek. "Night, Ma."

Pounder followed the boy into his room. The boy's room was small and sparsely furnished—his bed, a wardrobe, and a chair. As he kicked off his boots and changed into his nightshirt, he could hear his parents banking the fire for the night. The lamp light dimmed and went out. Tossing his clothes in a heap on the chair, Duane climbed into bed and sat with his knees tucked up under his chin.

The dog raised himself halfway onto the bed and pushed his muzzle under Duane's wrist. The boy stroked the muzzle and face, then tossled his ears gently with both hands.

"I love ya, Pounder," he said softly. The dog whined his own love for the boy. "Go ta bed, now, boy."

The large shadowy form slipped from the bed and curled itself into a comfortable position across the doorway.

Faint moonlight drifted in the window, casting a glow on the room. Duane sat there, his mind reeling, but blurred. He was tired. Pulling up the quilt, the boy settled down into the bed, closed his eyes, and drifted into sleep.

*   *   *

The sun stood high in a cloud-streaked sky. Before the afternoon was done, there would be a shower. The air was still and stuffy. The spring planting had been finished and the first shoots were showing, and buds were exploding into leaf as the trees awakened to the ending of April. Two and a half weeks had passed since the trip into town. The time was near for Andrew Kinkade to leave for the war which was fast brewing and would break as surely as the April storm building in the air.

The man stopped working out the weeds in the ground between the corn rows. For ten years he had worked the farm. As a lad of seventeen he had worked on a riverboat out of Ozark. Having met

25

Laura Blankenfield on a trip up from Little Rock, they eventually married and set up a store in Ozark. Looking for something further from the city filth, the Kinkades moved their business to Bendton. Duane was born in October of 1850. His parents decided to sell the store and take up farming. They liked being outdoors and felt farming would be a healthier way of life for Duane to grow up with.

Resting on his hoe handle, the worried man watched his son at work partway down the field. Barefoot and stripped to his waist against the sun's heat, Duane chopped expertly into the ground, separating the weeds from the earth. Sweat and dirt streaked his tanned and dirt-dusted body. A feeling of sadness washed through the father's mind and he longed to hold his son, to protect him, and to forget all about leaving for a war. A whisper of a breeze stirred his hair. He pondered the chore of preparing Duane to take over while he was gone. The war would be over by winter, but it still meant that the boy and his mother would have to harvest the crops and prepare the farm for winter while he was gone. And the idea did occur to him that he might not return. But it was a ridiculous thought and was dismissed from mind.

The clouds were billowing rapidly in rising mounds of white and grey and black. A few large drops of water fell, raising small dust clouds over dark, damp stains in the field's dirt.

"Dee," his father called, "storm's 'bout ta break. Time ta head fer the barn."

"Comin, Pa."

A flash of lightning chased the clouds across the sun, followed by rumbles of thunder and darkening skies. The storm broke as Duane caught up to his father.

"Storm's here, Pa." The boy reached his arm around his father's waist and felt the security of the strong, taut body, streaked with sweat, dust, and rain. This man, his pa, he was his tower of strength and his protection against the world. The downpour drenched the boy's hair and his trousers and he felt the clamminess of both plastered against his skin. He looked at his father's worried face, then leaned momentarily against the strong figure. A hand on his shoulder assured him his father sensed his feelings.

Once in the shelter of the barn, the tools were set by the door, then the man stood in the opening and watched the storm. Duane felt a drop of water strike the back of his shoulder and looked up toward the hole in the roof as a glare of light silhouetted it sharply for a split second and died out with an explosive crash. He joined his father, watching the wind drive sheets of water, and the explosive fireworks light up the world around them in dancing and ghostly visions.

A large form raced across the yard from somewhere beyond the garden as Pounder dashed toward the protection of the porch.

"Here, boy!" Duane called.

The dog changed direction mid-stride and flew into the barn. The boy and his father laughed as the drenched beast shook himself vigorously, then rolled in the dirt of the straw-strewn floor.

"Pa, I'm not ticklish taday."

Andrew's worried thoughts fell aside for the moment. "Is that a statement 'r a challenge?"

"A challenge."

The man reached down and lifted his son off the floor. Pounder jumped to his feet and started barking in playful, sharp yelps. Holding the boy around the waist with his left arm, Andrew ran the fingers of his free hand down Duane's ribs. The boy squirmed, but with both hands free, attacked his father's waist and ribs with merciless fingers. The sudden movement threw them off balance and they fell onto the straw-strewn ground. The dog danced in circles around the two. Tumbling about like a couple of puppies, they wore each other down, proving each to the other that he wasn't ticklish, each fending off the other's attack.

"Okay, Pa," Duane puffed, "I'm ticklish." They stopped, the man lying on his stomach; the boy having rolled to his knees to the side; the dog dropping to an alert crouch, ready to spring if the moment was right. There was a pause for each to catch his breath. Duane sat back on his heels. "Pa, when da ya leave?" he broke the quiet.

"End a the week, Son."

Andrew rolled over onto his back and Duane dropped down to lay close beside him. Pounder relaxed and lay down.

"What did I tell ya 'bout helpin yer Ma while I'm gone?"

"Do my chores 's usual, mend the fence . . . 'n the barn roof, 'n tend the crops 'n animals."

The storm died and the evening sun slanted its brightness through the cracks in the barn boards, casting patterns of light across the floor. Bars of light danced against the rain and dirt-streaked flesh of his pa's chest, face, and arms, as Duane sat up and laughed at the sight.

"Ya sure do look like sumthin, Pa. Like maybe Jamie's Pa got ya locked up."

"Maybe since the sun's back, we should finish thet piece a corn 'fer we stop ta supper." He pushed himself to his feet and started toward the glare of the doorway. Taking up his hoe from its place by the door, he stopped to await the boy.

"Comin, Pa." Duane scrambled to his feet. "Jest waitin ta be sure ya meant it."

As they returned to the field and continued to work the weeds from the rows, Pounder again took off to romp in the woods. An hour had passed when the two finally finished. Wearily they approached the barn, left their tools inside the door, and continued around to the pump to wash up.

Mrs. Kinkade greeted them from the doorway of the cabin. "I 'spect ya'll see ta gittin all thet dust 'n dirt off afer comin in. I put yer shirts on the pump." She waited until they disappeared around the corner of the building, then turned back into the house.

The boy and his father took turns pumping and splashing water over each other's bodies. A cake of soap on the edge of the water trough helped with the more stubborn dirt, ground into hands and elbows. Duane dried his head and arms briskly; then tossing the towel to his father, pulled on his collarless, homespun shirt.

Andrew did the same, leaving the towel spread on the pump handle to dry.

As they ascended the steps, Duane paused to call toward the wood lot. "Pounder! Come!"

There was a distant crashing as the dog burst into view and bounded toward the house. His coat was plastered with wet and mud where he had wallowed in the bottom land near the creek.

"Whoa, now," the boy warned. "Ya can't come in all a mess like thet! Go warsh up." He pointed toward the brook down the lane toward the road.

Pounder ambled off in the direction indicated.

Laura turned from the table as the two padded into the room. "Ya both must've been soaked in thet downpour. How fer did ya git?" she inquired.

"We done the sweet corn," Duane reported as he settled himself into his chair. "But we watched the storm from the barn."

His mother placed hot biscuits on the table as they all drew up their chairs. A plate of beef and a dish of garden beans and potatoes were already waiting.

They bowed their heads as his pa asked the blessing. "Dear Lord, bless this food we're 'bout ta eat 'n give us strength fer the hard times ahead. Amen."

"Andy, how much more da ya have ta do?" the woman asked as they helped themselves to the food.

"Afta supper, Dee 'n I'll walk the farm 'n go over ev'rythin ta be sure it's in order."

They ate quietly for several minutes before the man continued.

"We'll leave fer town tamorra mornin. We kin get what we'll need 'n make eny final 'rangements fer the summer items 'n fall sale a crops. The company forms up at two past noon. Ther'll be a parade 'n we'll camp east a town fer the night. Ya kin spend the night at Sally Rigg's boardin house 'n I'll see ya agin Saturday early 'fer we leave."

Duane finished a biscuit and drained his milk. "Pa, could I stay with ya tamorra night?"

"I'll check with Lieutenant Stanley. It should be okay. Da ya mind, Laura?"

"No. Thet's fine." She took the dishes to the drainboard.

The man and his son left the room. Pounder was waiting on the porch. He was wet, but clean of mud.

The woman turned to watch them stroll to the barn. The sun was nearing the western horizon. In another hour it would dip below for the night. A sudden surge of emotion and apprehension forced tears to her eyes. Wiping them away with the backs of her hands, she wondered, why did this war have to come? When he leaves he may never return. For another moment Laura stood watching, until her menfolk and the dog disappeared within the barn.

"Oh, God!" she prayed softly, "please, keep him safe. Bring him back ta us. We need him. We love him." She brushed new tears from her eyes, then returned to the table to finish clearing away the meal and its dishes.

Duane and his father walked through the barn looking to each tool and piece of equipment. Now and then they would stop while the man studied a harness or a corner, silently committing these moments with his son and these everyday sights to his memory—bidding a quiet farewell as though he might never see them again. Pounder sat in the doorway, a quiet sentinel,and watched the movement within. The sun had set and the twilight was fading as the three walked across the yard and up the steps to the front porch. They paused briefly, framed in the light of the open doorway, and watched together as the last rays of light faded from the western sky.

*　　*　　*

The wagon stood near the porch. The team was hitched and stood uneasy, waiting to be on the way. Duane knelt by his dog just outside the door, with his father's new uniform and blankets tied in a bundle, resting on the floorboards near his feet.

"Ya look afta thin's whilst we're gone. Ya hear, now, Pounder."

He stroked the head and neck, and scratched behind the ears. The dog sat quietly panting. He yawned, then licked the side of the boy's face in acknowledgment.

"Good, boy. Ya stay here now." He stood and looked to see if preparations were almost complete

His ma had a basket of food on the table and was tucking a cloth over the contents. His pa came from the bedroom with the shotgun and a pack of cartridges and percussion caps in hand.

"Laura, you 'r Dee may need this while I'm away. Ya neve' know what people might do in times like these." He hung the gun on the pegs over the fireplace and placed the cartridges and caps on the mantle. "Guess we're ready."

Duane picked up the bundle and climbed into the back of the wagon. His mother took the basket from the table. Andrew reached for his wife's arm and they walked out the door, closing it behind them. He helped her onto the wagon seat, then, climbing up beside her, took up the reins, and clucked the horses into motion. Pounder stood watching from the porch as the wagon rattled across the farm yard toward the dirt road beyond. There it paused while the man took one last look back at his home place. A thickness in his throat made it hard to swallow and moisture blurred his vision. Fighting back his emotions, Andrew started the horses again. The wagon rattled onward, leaving the farm behind, lost in a trailing cloud of dust.

*   *   *

The warmth of the morning sun radiated through the white canvass of the tent. As the drum beat the morning call, its cadence intruded on the man's dreams. He woke with a start, wondering at first what he was doing sleeping on the ground. Pushing off the rough wool blanket, he remembered, then looked to the figure sleeping beside him. Raising himself on his elbow, Andrew watched his son, still lost in a world of dreams. He smiled. How it hurt inside to know he would not see him until the Fall. The boy stirred. His father reached over and shook his shoulder gently.

"Dee, wake up."

"Huh?" He opened his eyes, squinting sleepily in a daze of half consciousness.

Mr. Kinkade wrapped him in his arms and pulled him close, tickling him through the blanket. The boy squirmed and struggled to free his arms, and struck back.

"Thet was a sneaky way ta do, Pa!"

"Don't matter, Son," he resisted the counterattack. "It got ya awake."

The attack was short-lived as the man hugged his son close and the boy squeezed back.

"Up 'n dress," Mr. Kinkade instructed. "They feed ya diff'rnt here then yer Ma does ta home."

Untangling themselves from the blankets, the two took the clothing that had been folded on their boots to serve as a pillow. Pulling on trousers and shirts, they jammed their feet into their boots, then sat up and finished dressing.

Duane briefly studied the man in his new uniform, then crawled through the tent flap. "Come on, Pa, I'm hungry."

He stepped out into the bustle of the camp with his father close behind. Men were headed toward the mess tent, some still tucking in shirt tails as they went.

"Dee, this way." Andrew pressed his son's arm to guide him in the right direction.

The cook tent was set near the center of the small camp. Nearly fifty youths and men gathered in line to take a tin plate, cup, and fork, then file past the cook table. Biscuits, ham, grits, and coffee were the morning fare. Once the plates were filled, each member of the troop found a place of his choosing to sit and eat. Duane and his father chose the tongue of a nearby wagon—the man settling on the main beam while his son perched on the cross tree.

Quiet conversation and a leisurely breakfast were interrupted with a new commotion as families joined their menfolk. Laura found Andrew and their son and joined them at the wagon.

"How'd ya sleep?" she asked, leaning against the wagon's wheel.

"Real good," Duane responded.

"Not bad," his father added, "but I'd rather be ta home." He finished a biscuit and sipped from his cup.

Duane chewed on a piece of ham. It was good to be together, all three of them. He became aware of the noise about them, of other families, of camp smoke, of horses. There was a feeling of family in a military encampment which signalled the separation of families.

The previous day's parade had been a fine showing of what the small town could do as a send-off for its menfolk.

A small band rendered the occasion musical and was joined by the crowd in a rousing rendition of DIXIE. The church women had fashioned a company flag and presented it to Captain Bellet. Little bundles of tailoring needs had been put together for each soldier, and food packets of baked goods and some cooked meat were given for the journey to Ozark. There were no weapons. During the last two weeks, most wives and mothers had fashioned a uniform of sorts for their menfolk. Each consisted of a light-blue pair of trousers with a broad yellow stripe down each side and a light, butternut brown shirt. More equipment was expected when the company reached the larger encampment at Ozark.

Morning drifted aimlessly along as the company's officers kept busy with meetings and organizational arrangements. The afternoon was spent learning drills and movements. Food supplies were loaded for the horses and the troops. Extra camp equipment and blankets were packed. The evening was spent with family and friends. As darkness deepened, the recruits drifted toward their tents.

Duane and his mother stood at the edge of the camp and watched their man walk off to its midst. They waved one last time as he disappeared into the cluster of humanity. The two stood close together for several minutes, then turned to walk back through town to Sally Riggs' place.

Saturday dawned clear and cool. The camp was up with the sun. By the time the townfolk were stirring, the camp had been taken down and the wagons were being loaded. The company prepared for an early departure in order to cover the twenty-three miles to Ozark by nightfall. Family and friends began to gather shortly after seven in the morning. Within the hour the company was fully packed and formed up for the march south. Loud cheering, last instructions from wives and mothers, and a plentiful mixing of tears sent them on their way. Many watched and waved for another quarter hour until the company disappeared over the last visible hill. A cloud of road dust hung on the hill's crest, then drifted away on the morning breeze.

Duane stood in the road with his mother, oblivious of all other people, aware only that a great aching emptiness hurt within his chest. He loved his father so much, and this grief he felt within was almost more than he could bear. Silent tears stung his eyes. He felt a drop of moisture on his wrist and suddenly realized his mother, too, was hurting. The boy slipped his arm around his mother's waist and she pulled him close in a loving embrace of common need and a mutual sense of deep loss. It was just the two of them now. Together they would survive this season of separation.

*   *   *

It was early afternoon as the wagon rattled across the small wooden bridge which spanned the brook that cut across the lane leading from the road to the farm yard. An extra horse was tied behind as its owner, Jamie Fowler, rode in the wagon bed with his friend, Duane. Eager barking echoed across the meadowland as Pounder bounded through the grass toward the inbound rig.

"Hey, Pounder!" the boy called.

"He sure has growd since I last saw him," Jamie observed.

"We'll git off here, Ma," Duane stated.

Laura slowed the team as the two boys jumped to the ground. They ran to meet an excited Pounder. The wagon moved on toward the house. The dog gathered himself midstride to leap at the boy and the two went down, rolling playfully in the grass. Mrs. Kinkade tied the team at the porch for the boys to help unload and put away. She proceeded with opening up the house and starting preparations for supper. The dog and the boys, having officially greeted one another, followed across the grass toward the house.

Knowing how hard the first days would be for her son and herself, Laura had invited Jamie to spend a week with them. His mother agreed it would be good for both families. Jonathan would be busy helping his town to adjust to the loss of its menfolk, and she and her daughters would be busy with the women's aid group preparing clothing and other supplies to send to the army. At ten years of age, Jamie was the youngest of three children. He could be a help to his mother and sisters, but the week away would be good for him as well as for his friend, Duane. The two had been close friends their entire lives as their families had known each other since the earlier years when the Kinkades had the general store. Jamie was the taller of the two and slightly heavier while Duane was the elder by six months.

"Race ya ta the wagon," Jamie challenged.

"Yer on!"

They broke into a fast run. The dog charged ahead, then slowed to keep pace. All three arrived together, though Jamie was the first to touch the spoke of the large rear wooden wheel. After catching their breath the boys began to carry the contents of the wagon into the house.

"Where d'ya want these, Mrs. Kinkade?" asked Jamie.

"Put ev'rythin ta the table," she replied. "I'll take care a them while you two tend the team."

After the wagon was unloaded, Duane led the team to the barnyard fence. The three horses were turned loose in the enclosure. Harnesses were taken in and hung on their pegs within the barn. Jamie's saddle and bridle were carried in and laid across the wooden rail of a box stall. Pounder was like a shadow. He followed each movement close at the boys' heels.

Dust particles danced in the beam of sunlight which intruded through the hole in the barn's roof.

"Thet's some hole ya got up there," Jamie observed.

"Yea," Duane acknowledged. "Pa says I need ta mend it whilst he's gone."

"Dee!" the voice called from the house.

The three hurried outside. "Yea, Ma," he responded.

"I need fresh water'n firewood," she stated.

"Okay!"

"I'll git the wood while yer fetchin water," Jamie offered.

"It's ov'r ther," Duane pointed. He turned to the house with the dog at his side.

*   *   *

The afternoon was spent catching up on chores and tending to the livestock. Following supper, the boys sat on the edge of the porch flooring and visited. Pounder lay napping close at Duane's side. Mrs. Kinkade cleaned up inside. When she finished she joined the boys outside, settling down at the top of the steps.

The three talked quietly for nearly an hour—Jamie sharing news of his family, Laura asking after his family's health and recent events in town, the boys speaking of plans for adventure, Mrs. Kinkade speaking of chores which should be included in their activity. Evening wore on and dusk came. The sun settled below the horizon and its light faded.

"Time fer bed," Mrs. Kinkade observed.

The four arose and stretched tired muscles. Pounder hopped down from the porch and trotted off toward the side yard for a drink from the water trough and a last run. The boys waited for him to return while Duane's mother banked the wood stove. The dog returned. The cabin door was closed for the night.

"Night, Ma." The boy kissed his mother's cheek and they embraced, each to reassure the other that it would be all right.

"Night, Son." She waited for the boys to turn in before she blew out the lamp and went to bed.

Jamie and Duane changed into night shirts, laying their clothes across the chair. Pounder settled across the doorway while the boys climbed into bed.

"Kinda tight fit," Jamie commented.

"Ya don't push me ta the floor 'n I'll not push you," Duane promised.

They settled down beneath the quilt, Jamie pulling his arms close to take as little space as possible, and Duane hanging part way out the side of the bed near the dog. A warm dampness licked at the back of his hand. His fingers searched for the soft chin and scratched gently.

"Dee?" Jamie whispered.

"Yea?" came the reply.

"How 'bout goin fishin tamorra?"

"Sounds good by me."

"Night."

"Night."

*   *   *

The early days of the week drifted leisurely, one into the next. Duane and Jamie tended the daily chores and worked the fields. Mrs. Kinkade was busy in the garden when not occupied with house chores or making a new uniform for her husband. The fishing trip of the first afternoon fizzled as the fish wouldn't bite. So the boys stripped off their clothing and went swimming instead. Pounder, too, enjoyed the swim. He joined them in their play with eager energy. However, when they were busy with chores, he either watched lazily from a comfortable vantage point or set out on an adventure of his own.

Mid-week continued to be bright and clear, yet cooler than the first two days. Morning chores were done and all had just finished breakfast when Duane spoke up.

"Ma, kin me 'n Jamie ride up ta Old Justin's place? It's a nice day fer ridin 'n we haven't seen him yet this spring."

Mrs. Kinkade was just gathering dishes from the table. "I reckon thet'd be all right. I'll give ya some a yest'rday's bread ta take to him."

The boys helped to clear the table.

"'Fore ya go," Laura continued, "fetch up the laundry tub 'n extra water. 'N bring yer dirty clothes so's I kin warsh whilst yer gone."

"Yes'm," Duane replied.

The two hurried to do as asked. Meanwhile, Mrs. Kinkade wrapped a loaf of bread in a flour sack and tied a piece of line around the top to hang it from the saddle. Outside, the metallic clatter heralded the movement of the wash tub from its peg on the side of the house to the front porch. After a period of quiet while away at the pump, the boys came clambering up the steps with two buckets of water. They placed them on the floor, just inside the door. Mrs. Kinkade handed Duane the sack as she kissed him lightly on the cheek.

"You all be careful, now," she said.

"We will," Jamie assured.

"See ya by suppertime," Duane added.

The two walked to the barn with the dog dancing excitedly alongside. Mrs. Kinkade filled a large kettle and placed it on the stove. Glancing out the door for any sign of activity, she crossed to the bedroom and gathered the dirty clothing from the chair, the floor, and the bedpost. Returning to the main room she stepped out onto the porch and deposited the collection in the empty tub. She remained waiting for the boys to finish saddling their horses and to start on their way. The horses had been led from the barnyard and tied at the fence rail. They were ready except for tightening the cinch straps. With final adjustments completed, stirrups were dropped and the horses untied and turned toward the house. The boys mounted and rode first to the porch.

"We'll be goin now, Ma," Duane stated.

"Ya both look afta each other," she smiled. "Pounder, ya see they keep safe, ya hear."

A sharp bark acknowledged the instruction.

Mrs. Kinkade watched as the boys reined their mounts toward the front lane and the dog raced ahead. Pounder splashed through the brook as the horses clopped across the bridge deck. He raced on to the road where he sat and waited to see which way his master would turn. The riders turned north and disappeared around a small hill. The woman turned back into the house to check the water heating on the stove.

Justin Pierce's place was about six and a half miles up the road. He lived alone, a bearded bachelor of fifty-some years. Periodically he would stop at the Kinkade farm to visit, and always he would show up to help with the harvest.

Duane and his father always helped Justin when his crops were ready for harvest. On occasion he would join them and ride into town for staple goods or other supplies. Yet, for the most part, he was a loner and kept to himself.

The boys were in no hurry. They enjoyed letting the horses amble along at a slow walk while Pounder departed on small scouting trips to chase a rabbit or follow a scent. There were several small farms along the way and twice they waved at a distant figure, busy in the fields. Grasshoppers flitted about the tall grass. Butterflies and bees busied themselves on wildflower blossoms. An occasional bird filled the air with song in harmony with the constant waves of vibrant noise from the katydids. They paused at a bubbling stream for the horses to drink and to quench their own thirsts, then rode on.

As they neared the end of the journey, they came upon a quarter-mile stretch of straight road.

"Race ya ta thet hill crest," Jamie challenged.

"The horses 'r tired," Duane observed.

"It's not but a short run," the younger boy offered.

"Okay," Duane accepted. "Go!"

Pounder was startled by the sudden charge into a dead run and bolted into motion alongside. Then something caught his ear and he suddenly cut in front of the racing pair. Jamie's horse turned to avoid the dog as Duane reined his mount to the side to prevent a collision. The younger boy, caught completely unaware, went flying from his saddle. He struck the ground hard and rolled wildly through the grass. The reins hung free and the horse stopped to graze. Duane brought his horse up short, dropping his reins as he jumped to the ground. He approached the still figure, lying unconscious in the tall grass, already tended to by the soft whines of the dog who lay at his side washing the dirt from his face with gentle passes of the large tongue.

The dark curly hair was a tangle of dirt and weeds, grass and wildflower. Streaks of red and ground-in dirt marred the side of the boy's face. His clothing was stained with brown and green, the soft red of sparse bleeding, and was torn in several places.

Duane knelt beside his friend. He was breathing. There was no significant sign of serious injury. But he lay so still and quiet-like.

"Why, Pounder?" he inquired of the dog. "Why'd ya cut us off 'n git Jamie hurt?"

The dog responded by taking gentle hold of his master's hand and tugging lightly. He let go and started to walk away. Duane was puzzled and did not move. The dog repeated his request.

"Ya want me ta folla?" The boy stood.

Pounder ran ahead toward the hill, but avoided the road. Duane followed. Climbing the hill, the dog stopped just below the crest and lay down. The boy approached cautiously. Suddenly he heard it—gunfire and shouting, and another noise he could not distinguish. Stealthily he crept to the hilltop and peered at the scene beyond.

Justin's place lay a half mile ahead. The boy could barely make out a group of riders in a frenzy of shouting and shooting, working their horses in small circles. The other sound, he observed, was the roar of flames as they consumed the structures of the small farm. A panic of fear surged through the boy's stomach and he felt a rising sickness. He had to do something before there was a chance of being discovered.

The two hurried back to Jamie. Duane dropped beside his friend and called frantically, "Jamie! Jamie! Wake up!" He shook a shoulder. "Jamie! Ya okay?"

Slowly, the boy began to stir. "Ohhh," he moaned softly. He opened his eyes and stared at Duane. "What happened? I hurt all ov'r."

"Yer horse threw ya," Duane answered. "Enythin broke?"

"Can't feel nothin," Jamie responded. "Dunno yet." He tried to sit up. "Ev'rythin seems ta work." He rose into a seated position.

"We gotta git outa here," Duane's voice was urgent. "There's raiders ahead. They're burnin Justin's place."

Jamie's brown eyes clouded briefly with pain. He caught a quick breath to keep from crying out, then relaxed.

"What hurt?" his friend asked.

"Ev'rythin." He continued to work himself to his hands and knees, then with help from Duane, he pushed himself to his feet. "I think I'm jest banged 'n bruised. Nothin seems broke."

"Kin ya ride?"

"Yea."

The dog started ahead, circling through the meadow around the hill, heading toward a stand of trees. Duane helped his friend onto his horse, then mounted his own. The two followed. By the time they arrived at a safe spot to view the destruction, the raiders had departed. The sound of galloping hoofbeats faded northward leaving the crackling fire and silence. Cautiously the boys rode into the farmyard. What livestock remained had been slaughtered. The buildings were reduced to crackling embers and white smoke. There was no sign of Mr. Pierce.

"We gotta warn the others," Duane stated.

"I gotta tell Pa," Jamie added.

Pounder searched about the wrecked farm, following and exploring scents which were new and confusing. Finally he sorted out what he was looking for and followed it down the lane a short distance. He would know these raiders if they came again. Suddenly he turned and ran barking toward the trees on the far side of the yard as a single figure leading a horse came into view.

"It's okay, boy!" Duane called. "Mr. Pierce! Over here!"

The man recognized the boys and hurried to where they waited. He was unhurt, but very angry.

"Ya okay?" Jamie called.

"Damn right, I'm okay!" he called. "They was here when I come up 'n I knew this weren't the time ta face em." As he approached, he noticed Jamie's disheveled appearance. "What happened ta you, boy?"

"My dog caused his horse ta throw 'im. He was tryin ta warn us so's we wouldn't git caught."

Pounder returned to sit near Duane's foot.

"Mighty smart dog, Dee." Justin gathered the reins and mounted his horse. "This the same pup I saw last fall?"

"The same."

"Sure did a heap a growin." He guided the horse to turn and face the destruction.

"Kin we do enythin ta help?" Jamie asked.

"Don't appear nothin's left," the old man stated. "We best head fer town 'n warn folks along the way." He reined his mount toward the road.

The small party turned to follow and began the trip homeward. They rode much of the way at an easy walk since the boys' horses had not had a chance to rest. Warning was given at each farm along the way. Upon arriving home, the three sat down at the kitchen table and gave a full report to Mrs. Kinkade. Mr. Pierce was invited to spend the night. He would go on to town to report to the marshall. Jamie would stay on as originally arranged and the family would ride into town on Saturday.

Laura took the shotgun down and removed two cartridges from their pack. Each barrel was loaded and tamped and the gun was returned to its place. Two caps were removed from their tin and placed conveniently on the mantle.

*   *   *

An overcast sky gave a dingy cast to the afternoon air. The little brook bubbled noisily along its course through the meadow. Pounder lay on the wooden planks that spanned the water and watched the barefoot boys, stripped of their shirts, gathering up stones from the stream bed.

"How deep ya think we kin make this water?" Jamie inquired as he dumped his armful onto the pile already begun on the brook's embankment.

"It should come as high as the bank," Duane believed. They had selected the lower edge of a quiet pool as their dam site. Here the brook was narrow and the embankment was about two feet high on either side. For a half hour they had been gathering stones from along the stream's bed and piled them near the selected work site.

"Guess this oughta be 'nough," Duane observed.

"I'll hand em ta ya," his friend offered.

Construction began. The first stones were passed from the pile and placed in the water. As the cut was filled with the collection of stone, the boys noted with disappointment that the water just passed through the pile.

"It's not holdin much a enythin," Jamie complained.

"Maybe the stones aren't big 'nough," Duane suggested.

"Dee, here's a real big one out here in the grass."

Hidden amidst the wildflowers, Jamie had discovered a large rock, bigger than any they had found as yet. It measured nearly three feet from end to end. Using a shovel they had brought from the barn, the two struggled to remove the rock from the ground. Pounder came to help dig. He worked on one side while the boys worked on the other. Finally it was loosened. Even so, it was so large as to require the shovel as a lever and the combined weight

43

of both boys to pry it from the ground. With much effort, they rolled it to the edge of the bank and toppled it into the water. It fell with a loud crunch, wedging itself among the smaller stones. Yet, still, the water did not rise.

The dog stood on the far bank and watched as the boys finally exhausted their supply of building material.

"Why not shovel dirt 'n clay from the bank into the stones?" Jamie suggested.

"Worth a try," Duane agreed.

Part of the bank was cut away from below the construction site and the dirt shoveled behind the stone work.

"It's workin," Duane observed.

The water began to rise. Then, as the pressure grew from the rising water, the dirt began to wash away.

"Darn, thet's not workin neither," Jamie complained.

The dog started digging along the top of the bank, sending dirt, grass, and weeds into the water's flow.

"Look," Jamie pointed, "the grass is helpin ta hold the dirt."

Duane cut small chunks of sod from the meadow grasses. He passed them to Jamie who, in turn, dumped them upside-down onto the stones. It worked. The structure began to hold water. The two worked at a feverish pace until the stone and sod construction was well over a foot in height.

"Look's good, Jamie," the older boy commented.

"Let's see how deep it gits," the other suggested.

The two boys and the dog gathered on the bank, just upstream from their project, and sat to watch for results.

Distant thunder rumbled in the sky. Jamie rubbed absent-mindedly at the scabbed-over scratches on his cheek from the accident of two days back. Duane brushed the dirt from his hands onto his trousers. The water continued to rise as their structure continued to hold. A sudden rush of air chilled their naked backs and the boys shivered in its coolness. Raindrops splashed on their shoulders and dampened their hair as they fell, too, on the brook's surface, sending ever-widening rings wavering outward. Pounder shook his head.

Lightning danced across the sky and thunder crashed.

"Guess we'd best head in," Jamie suggested.

"Let's wait a bit 'n see how our dam works," Duane protested.

The air hummed, then split with a blinding flash and an explosive crash as a bolt of lightning struck a tree on the hill out near the road. The storm burst upon them in a heavy deluge and each was instantly drenched through.

"Let's go!" Jamie screamed.

The boys fled to the protection of the porch with the dog right on their heels. Duane's mother met them at the door.

"Don't ya two have 'nough sense ta come in fer it rains!" she exclaimed. "Ya'll ketch yer death in this. An look at you, Pounder. Yer bad as these boys here!" She shook her head. "Ya strip outa them wet thin's right here, then wrap up in some'thin dry by the fire."

While Jamie and Duane peeled off their wet trousers and johns, Mrs. Kinkade rummaged through a blanket chest for two flannel bed sheets. She shook them open and wrapped one around each naked child as he entered the room, and herded him over by the hearth.

"You wait!" she ordered as the dog started through the door.

Pounder sat, forlorn and dripping, while she went in search of an old worn blanket. She returned instead with a worn towel and an armful of flour sacks. Pounder stood and shook himself.

"Com'on in," she called. "Git ther' by the fire," she pointed. Throwing the towel to Duane, his mother explained, "Dee, lay this out fer yer dog, then rub him down with these flour sacks." She tossed the sacks to Jamie.

Duane worked with the sheet draped over his shoulders and managed to direct his dog to lie down on the towel. Meanwhile, his mother stirred up the fire and added three more sticks to fuel it. While Jamie passed the sacks to Duane, Laura closed the door against the storm and took a seat on the floor between the boys. She used the edge of Jamie's sheet and vigorously rubbed the moisture from his hair while her son used the sacks to dry his dog. When she was satisfied that Jamie's head was sufficiently dry, she went to work on her son's. Neither boy protested. She was gentle, and the warmth of the fire felt good as it warmed the sheets and dried their skin. Pounder rolled over on his back to enjoy his drying rubdown, then shifted to his belly, resting his chin on his forepaws. The damp sacks were tossed into a pile on the hearthstone where the fire's heat began to steam the dampness from them.

Thin wisps of vapor drifted from the fabric as well as from the dog's coat. Outside, the storm howled and buffeted the roof. Lightning flashed and thunder crashed. Laura rubbed the sheet against Duane's arms and back. There was a peace wrapped in the comfort of the sheet and the warmth of the fire. There was a security in his mother's presence and the boy leaned back into her arms. She held him tenderly, folding her arms around this precious son and holding him close. Jamie snuggled up close on her other side and she took him also into her embrace. As she sat there holding the two boys close and felt their sense of security and that moment of peace and the presence of love and trust, as she stared with the two of them and the dog at the flames dancing merrily and in comforting warmth, as she sat there and listened to the violence of the storm outside; she was struck with the irony in the quiet security they had at this moment in contrast to the uncertain and unknowing absence of her husband. Somewhere there was a war unfolding. It seemed so unreal! God, how she missed him!

"Ma?" Duane gazed blankly beyond the flames to some distant place in his mind.

"Yes, Son."

"Do ya miss Pa?"

She held him closer and touched her chin to the top of his head. "I miss yer Pa very much, Dee. I miss him so much thet it aches me inside."

There was a moment of quiet. Even the storm was beginning to subside so that the crackle of the fire dominated the mind.

"I love ya, Ma."

"I love ya, too, Dee." Tears stung the woman's eyes. A sudden thickness filled her throat. She wanted to cry, but fought instead to control her emotion.

"Mrs. Kinkade?"

"Yes, Jamie," she rasped, her voice broken by her feelings.

"If'n ya was my Ma, I'd love ya, too."

She smiled. "Thank ya, Jamie." The emotion passed to a sense of humor tickling in her train of thought. "Ya boys best be thinkin a gittin inta a change a clothes ta do the chores. I'm gonna git started with som'thin ta eat."

Duane rolled forward and sprawled on the floor beside Pounder. Jamie crawled into the rocking chair and tucked his knees in close to his chin. Mrs. Kinkade pushed herself to her feet and turned toward the stove. The storm had dwindled to a soft drizzle and the woman wandered to the door to look out across the fields.

"Dee, Jamie, come look!" she called as she stepped out onto the porch.

The boys and the dog rushed to the doorway to see what the excitement was about.

"I neve seen the front meada flooded so," Laura remarked.

Duane dropped a corner of the sheet to free his arm and pointed to a spot below the bridge. "Look!" he exclaimed. "Our dam musta worked! See the hole where the water falls away?" The others looked and acknowledged. "Thet's where we built the dam this aftanoon."

"Yea," agreed Jamie. "With the storm 'n all, it musta got more water 'n it could let through."

The flow of water boiled over the top of the stones and the edges of the embankment to either side, backing over twenty feet into the field beyond either bank of the brook. The clouds passed and a brightness of late afternoon sun flooded the yard as the drizzle faded to nothing. No more was said as the boys and Pounder turned back through the door toward the bedroom. Mrs. Kinkade picked up the wet clothing from its pile on the floorboards and stepped to the edge of the porch to ring it out. Then she, too disappeared into the house.

* * *

At week's end, the wagon was hitched up and the farm was left in the care of the dog. The trip to town was uneventful, yet informative. Laura arranged to have a dagguereotype made of her and Duane. The small photographic image was enclosed in a closing frame to be sent with their letters to Andrew. The first mail had arrived and included a letter which had been hastily written and posted in Ozark. It was brief, stating the man's love for his family and providing information on how their letters should be sent. The company's immediate destination was Little Rock. There it would become part of the larger force already engaged in training and outfitting in preparation for assignment as needed.

The afternoon was spent at the Fowler's. For the children it was a time of play, mostly hide-and-seek.

Their parents spoke of the war and of the threat caused by marauding raiders who were entering the northwestern part of the state from western Missouri. Perhaps it would be best for the Kinkades to bring their livestock and move in with one of the families on the edge of town. But Laura didn't want that just yet. She and her son had to take care of the place for Andrew. They would, however, keep the option open should the danger reach a crisis.

The boy and his mother retired to the boarding house for the night. They each wrote a letter to Private Andrew Kinkade. The following morning the picture and the letters were wrapped in a small paper packet and posted at the stage depot to go with the mail destined for the army camps at Little Rock. It was Sunday, so they attended services at the community church and departed toward home after dinner.

Weeks dragged into months. The season slipped into summer. The crops grew. The boy and his dog wandered the hills, went swimming, maintained the little dam which began to improve in effectiveness as silt and debris from summer storms built up behind the stonework. Periodically Jamie might spend a few days or he and his father would stop on their way to visit the outlying farms. From time to time the Kinkades would spend a day or two in town. The chores were done, the crops were cared for, socks were mended, letters were written. The mail traveled slowly and erratically, but gradually Duane and his mother learned of his father's life in the army. There was also news of the opening battles of a war which was expected to be over by the autumn harvest.

On May 6, 1861, Arkansas adopted an Ordinance of Secession and the Confederate Congress recognized the existence of war between the United States and the Confederate States.

As Spring gave way to Summer, preparations increased in intensity. States of the Confederacy seized properties, stores, fortifications, and remaining troops from the Federals. To the west, competition was underway to gain control of the Indian Territory. Officers were appointed and troops were prepared. The advancing season saw increased activity in naval engagements and some skirmishes along the coast and in the East. July saw an accelerating pace of skirmishes and engagements of troops in Missouri and northwestern Arkansas as troops fought for control of Missouri. By mid month the Union had assembled an army and was advancing toward Manassas, Virginia. Throughout the third week, Confederate forces were also massing along Bull Run near Manassas.

As July drew to a close, the boy and his mother had heard of the battle at Manassas and had become aware of a general realization that the war would not be as quickly decided as had once been thought. Word came that a brigade of state troops under a General Pearce was joining with a General McCulloch with more Arkansas troops and troops from Missouri, en route to engage the Union forces near Springfield. It was unclear as to the whereabouts of the company from Bendton.

*   *   *

The dog padded through the open door into the kitchen and plopped noisily beside the table. Laura listened as she worked at the stove, for the footsteps that followed behind. Duane walked carefully to the table where he set the dipper of milk from the morning's chores. The air sizzled with the fragrance of eggs frying. The boy approached the stove to glance into the skillet and to be near his ma.

"Smells good," he observed.

She tossled his hair affectionately. "Almost done."

He turned to a nearby shelf and took down a glass pitcher. Returning to the table, he emptied the milk into the container.

"Ma?" Duane began as he poured the milk.

"Yes?" She didn't turn from the stove.

"Afta brekfist, me 'n Pounder wanta ride over ta the Pryor's farm 'n see if they's heard enythin 'bout the Bendton Company from their sons." He turned and set the empty container on the drainboard.

"There's chores ta be doin round here this mornin." She set the platter of eggs and cornbread on the table. "Wait till afta noon. Remember yer Pa said the gate ta the barnyard needs fixin as does the hole in the roof." She reached her hand behind his head and pulled him gently along. "Now sit up ta yer brekfist fer it gits cold."

They sat to the table and Duane said grace. As they ate, they spoke of plans to get help for the harvest and prepare for winter. It had become obvious that the war was not ending, but expanding. Duane shared some of his cornbread with the dog who kept an expectant eye out for anything that might come his way, on purpose or accidental. A piece of egg which slipped from the fork was caught mid-air before reaching the floor.

When Duane had finished, he took his dishes to the drainboard. A dusty stray beam of sunlight drifting in through the window fell on the plate, highlighting the glazed pattern. The boy's gaze fell on the pattern and he followed it absentmindedly with his finger. Having slowly passed the finger over the eggy surface, he turned it up and stared at the yellow slime.

Mrs. Kinkade finished her coffee and returned the empty cup to its saucer. She turned to watch her son's play as Pounder stood, stretched and walked to his side. After a minute, she broke the silence.

"The work ain't gittin done of itself."

"Yea, Ma." He offered the finger to his dog who eagerly licked it clean.

"Dee!"

"It were dirty," the boy alibied as he turned quickly toward the door and darted out.

Duane flashed through the air with the dog flying on ahead as he flew off the porch to the ground, avoiding all three steps. His dark hair whipped about in the breeze of flight. Landing squarely on bare feet, he stopped short and glanced at the rough blue sky spattered recklessly with white puffs of cotton-like clouds. The morning light sparkled in his brown eyes as his line of sight fell to the roof line of the barn, that squat structure with its weathered coat of paint and the hole in the middle of the roof where the wind had blown off the shingles in a late winter storm. The boy stood in the middle of the yard for a moment with his hands in his pockets and stared at that hole.

A sharp barking reminded him that the dog was ready for some kind of adventure.

"Hey, Pounder. Come 'ere, boy." The dog hurried back from the shadow of the barn and the boy knelt to give him a rough rubbing on his neck.

Duane stood and slowly approached the barn doors which stood slightly ajar. Pounder followed as he inserted the toes of his foot in the crack between the two doors and pulled one open just enough to squeeze through. The boy stood inside the door with his hands jammed back into his pockets, and gazed at the hole from the underside. Pounder eased himself into a sitting position and waited. Then the boy led and the dog followed as the two surveyed the barn's interior with an eye for likely spots in which there might be some shingles. Along the wall to the right were three box stalls, empty as the stock was out to pasture, with bridles hanging from the corner posts and two saddles on wooden horses in front. Near the back door was a heap of wood scraps. In the back of the barn to the left were two standing stalls. Along the left wall were the feed bins and the stacked sacks of grain. Also along that wall were the harnesses, a work bench, and tools racked on the wall. Cabinets and shelves were along the front wall. In the center of the floor was a pile of hay, while some barrels, crates, and tools lay scattered about the rest of the floor space.

Duane strolled over to the scrap pile near the back door and investigated it with a kick. Pounder dug hesitantly, not knowing what was wanted. Perhaps there were some shingles if he looked. Glancing about for something to sit on while he searched through the wood scraps, he spied a small empty crate near the box stalls. Approaching it, he stepped gingerly on the top edge of one side to turn the opening toward him, carefully hooked an inside corner with a toe, and swung it into the air toward the scrap pile. Pounder, who was still pawing through the debris, barked sharply and jumped to the side as the crate bounced near his side. The boy finished positioning the seat, withdrew his hands from his pockets, and sat down to sort. One by one he picked up the wood pieces and chucked them behind him, and would have succeeded in scattering the pile, except that the dog kept picking them up and fetching them to the boy's side. But there were no shingles. Placing chin in hand, Duane sat there and stared at Pounder. The dog cocked his head to the side and stared back.

"Nothin here, boy. Guess the roof'll hafta wait." After a moment, he stood up, thrusting his hands into his pockets, and called, "Come on, Pounder. We'll take one last look fer quittin."

They walked first along the box stalls, looking into each as they passed. Approaching the pile of hay in the middle, they kicked and pawed it into oblivion. Still no shingles. It really didn't matter. He wasn't in any mood to climb up onto the roof. Maybe he could fix the gate first and do the roof another time. The two reached the door. Duane pushed it open with his foot and they passed outside to survey the fence.

Shuffling first to a position about ten feet from the gate, Duane squatted in the dirt with both elbows on his knees, his chin in his hands, and his head tilted slightly to one side. The dog dropped down beside him to wait. From this vantage point they watched the sagging gate, almost as though they expected it to tell them why it sagged. Suddenly the boy saw why. The rope—running from the tall post to which the gate was hinged, to the outer end of the gate—was broken, causing the end to rest on the ground. All he had to do to fix it was to find a piece of rope with which to replace the broken one.

The dog whined as if to say, how much longer before we can do something interesting?

"This won't take long, boy." The boy stroked his friend's heavy coat. "Ya jest lay here a bit. I'll say when it's done."

Pounder yawned, then lay on his belly to watch and wait. The boy thought a bit longer. After a moment's concentration he recalled a coil of line hanging on the far side of the barn. Using this, he first secured one end to the end of the gate, then took the other and climbed the fence to tie it to the top of the post. But one problem presented itself. The gate was too heavy to lift from where he was working so that he could tie the rope to the post. Surveying the problem from where he stood, it became evident that he would have to prop the fence up somehow. Some scraps of wood solved the problem and shortly afterwards the gate swung freely.

Gee, that sure was easy, he thought. He looked back toward the barn roof and studied it thoughtfully for about five seconds. Then tossing the wood blocks aside, Duane shrugged his shoulders in a the-heck-with-it way and turned down the back lane toward the back meadow where the fishing hole was.

"Come on, Pounder. Let's go."

The dog jumped up to follow and they quickly disappeared beyond the tall crop in the corn field.

The sun winked quietly on the cool rippling water as the boy and the dog ran across the sloping meadow toward the deep pool in the creek near the shadow of the oak tree. Duane dropped down in the hot sunlight at the pool's edge. Pounder ran splashing into the shallows where the rocks were. The day felt warm and the water looked inviting. The grass was cool and felt good against his bare arms. A fish broke the surface nearby as if to say, come on in; and the boy watched him play within the depths of the dark pool. Soon he found that he was staring at himself in his reflection on the surface of the water, so he made a few faces until one satisfied him. Rolling over onto his back, Duane stared at the blue, white-splashed sky and felt the sun dance on his face. Gee it felt warm. Maybe he'd take a short dip.

Springing to his feet, the boy quickly scattered his clothes on the ground around him and, with a quick step, leaped into the pool. The moment of impact snapped and he felt himself suspended momentarily beneath the water before he broke through into the air. The coolness was great. So for the next few hours he became a fish and explored the water's depths, just missed getting eaten by a coon, had a near brush with a fisherman, was saved from numerous imaginary disasters when his dog splashed out to the rescue, and lost all track of time.

Darkening skies interrupted his images of adventure and he decided it was time to head for home. A sudden breeze kicked up and a dampness invaded the air. Thunder rumbled in the distance and an occasional flash sparked the clouds. The rain began as Duane touched the shore and it occurred to the boy that it might be just as much fun to run about and soak up the wet drops. The dog climbed out on the bank beside him and shook vigorously to rid himself of excess water. Duane closed his eyes tight and laughed as the spray struck his body and his face. He could feel rivulets of moisture running down his neck and back, arms and legs. A light rush of air chilled the skin and sent shivers through the boy's body. Slipping on his johns, Duane picked up the remainder of his clothing and carried it as he struck out toward the house at a slow and easy walk. Pounder followed at his side, stopping every now and then to shake off the extra moisture of the rainfall.

The storm quit as quickly as it had begun. By the time the boy and his dog crossed into the farmyard, the sun was breaking clear and sparkling about the damp yard. A quiet settled on the farm and the boy paused to feel it. Pounder took the opportunity to roll in the grass while Duane pulled on his trousers, slipped into his shirt, and wiped the dirt from his feet before starting toward the porch. He had been gone longer than he had planned. It was well past midday. As he straightened up, the boy caught the sound of horses, several of them, rushing up the road approaching the farm. The dog stopped mid-roll and jumped to his feet, barking wildly. In the air was a faint hint of that scent from an earlier experience.

Like a flash Duane was on the porch and in the house. The dog followed on his heels, barking wildly, hackles raised.

"Ma! Ma! Raiders!"

Mrs. Kinkade gazed at her son in momentary disbelief before moving toward the hearth to get the shotgun. Pulling back both hammers, she placed the caps on their nipples, then carefully lowered the hammers to rest on them. With fear and determination she crossed the threshold to meet whoever was coming, on the porch and with barrel leveled. Her dark cotton dress blew slightly in the breeze of late afternoon. She stood firm with face set and eyes dark and angry.

"Ya stay back, ya hear now!" she instructed her son.

Duane nodded to her back but said nothing. Remaining in the cabin, he knelt beside the dog and restrained him from charging through the open door.

Seven men rode full tilt into the farm yard with guns drawn. Their horses were lathered from hard riding and they themselves were matted with dirt and sweat. Reining to a halt facing the woman, they said nothing, only laughed when she told them to get out. Several shots rang out as she flew backwards against the wall and slumped to the floor. They looked at one another and roared with laughter, then proceeded to pick out targets throughout the yard until they had emptied their guns. Turning their attention to the barn, they started gathering whatever they could take.

The cackling hens scattered about the flying hooves of the prancing horses. Frantic squawkings added to a sense of fear and confusion as individual raiders dismounted, grabbed the birds by the neck, and swiftly executed them. Dead poultry was passed to mounted members of the band who tied them to leather thongs hanging on their saddles. Two of the group were using their ropes and horses to tear down fencing and to pull the wagon over on its side.

Busy at killing and destroying, the raiders did not notice the boy with glazed eyes of disbelief. He remained motionless within the house, frozen by fear and shock, while the commotion unfolded outside. His grasp slipped and the dog broke free. Pounder dashed wildly through the door, gathered the power within every muscle of motion to spring from the porch at the closest rider. The startled killer reached for his revolver. Before it was clear of the holster, the heavy bulk of wild fury struck the man carrying him to the ground. Instinctively the dog sank his teeth into the unprotected throat. An eruption of blood bathed the dog and man with a red flow of death, as the two struck the ground and rolled in the damp earth. The impact broke the deathgrip. The dog rolled free of the corpse, momentarily disoriented.

Still in a daze, Duane stood in the open door, staring at the floundering dog. He turned and saw the crumpled body beside the door. The boy moved mechanically slow, to stand by his mother's side, to stare at the unreal. Then it struck him.

"Ma? Ma!!" he screamed as he dropped beside her, blinded by bitter tears. The shotgun rested in lifeless hands.

As some of the riders turned in reaction to their fallen comrade and the sudden scream, the blood-splattered dog regained his footing and the boy took the gun to stand and face his enemies.

"Hey! Over here!" one called.

They turned, caught off guard, to face a bloodied beast and the screaming boy with shotgun leveled at them. His face was tear-streaked, but his eyes were dry with a crazed look about them.

"You killed her!!" he cried. "Murderers!! Damn ya ta Hell!!" The voice shrieked uncontrollably as his thumbs pulled back the twin hammers.

The remaining six grabbed for their guns as the boy's piece spoke loudly twice. But the revolvers were empty. One grabbed his leg and doubled up in pain as his horse screamed and reared, twisting wide-eyed, struck by part of the blast. A second rider was blown to the ground, struck through the chest with the full force of the charge.

Three of those remaining drew saddle rifles as the dog raced across the yard and leaped once more to the attack. Shots rang out. A boot caught the dog on the side of the head. As Pounder flipped sideways in mid-flight, the boy flew back against the porch post. The dog's body hit the dirt and tumbled toward the corner of the porch. The gun slipped from Duane's grip and fell down the steps as his head exploded in pain. A burning sensation invaded his chest and blackness clouded his consciousness as he collapsed forward, falling from the wooden floor into the rain-wet grass.

Reddish dampness soaked the boy's dark hair and washed down the side of the pale face, collecting into a pool in the dirt. A widening red seeped through the fabric of the shirt as it flowed from a hole near the side of his chest. The small body lay still and deathlike in its pooling blood.

Quickly the riders sheathed their rifles and wheeled their horses around toward the barn. The haystack was fired. Brands of burning stalk were used to ignite the barn. A burning brand of wood was thrown through the open door of the cabin as the remaining raiders hastened to depart toward the road. Galloping hooves faded down the lane as flames crackled from the barn and the burning haystack.

Dampness still hung on the late afternoon air from the earlier shower, and the sun glistened brightly on its journey approaching the horizon. The crickets chattered noisily from the undergrowth. The horses, the cow and her calf wandered in from the back pastureland. They stopped to graze by the garden. An eerie silence hung about the farm, broken by crickets, crackling flames, and contented munching of the large animals.

Stunned, but unhurt, the dog whined in pain as he slowly pushed himself to his feet. His nose caught the scent of fire in the cabin as he hopped awkwardly onto the porch and limped in the direction of the door. Retrieving the torch from within, he emerged from the room with the burning wood clamped in his teeth. Pounder paused briefly, dazed and uncertain, then walked to the edge of the flooring and dropped it in the grass.

The dog turned to the still form that was his master. He licked the blood from the pale face. The skin was warm. He whined his plea for some response, some movement. There was none. Pounder lay down beside his helpless friend, resting his muzzle protectively on a bloodied hand. There he remained until dusk.

The evening light began to fade as the sun dipped below the horizon and a deep blue-black began to reach across the heavens from the east. Pounder had not moved from the boy. There had been no change, no movement, for nearly four hours. The barn was gone. Only wisps of white smoke and a glow of read embers marked where it had stood. The livestock had moved to the front meadow near the brook. In the darkness of nightfall, a broken moon cast its dim glow on the countryside and dark forms of the horses and cattle revealed where they had settled down for the night's sleep.

The dark canopy with its twinkling vastness was complete. Quiet sounds of night, the tree toads and crickets, wrapped the silence of death and destruction. The soft light of the moon caressed the bodies that lay in the farmyard and about the porch of the cabin. The dog stirred.

Whining softly, he nudged the small form beside him, pleading for the boy to wake up. Still, no response. Pounder sat up and howled mournfully at the moon. The ghostly cry echoed in the night air. Finally, the dog stood, made one last attempt to rouse his master, then walked off across the yard out the front lane. Crossing the wooden bridge, he broke into a loping run as he faded into the night along the road to Bendton.

*   *   *

The white clapboard house stood behind a low picket fence on a side street near the eastern end of town. In the fading light and long shadows of a moon nearing the end of its night's passing, a dark shape padded across the weedy grass of the side yard and sprung upon the porch.

Scratching at the door and barking wildly, Pounder sought to get the attention of Duane's friend, Jamie. When the door creaked open, it was the boy's father who peered out at the dog with blood-crusted coat, barking wildly with a mixture of mournful and pleading whines.

"What's there, Pa?" the boy called from his bedroom door within.

"It's yer friend's dog, 'n he's all bloodied," the father replied. "Fetch a lamp, Son."

The man took the dog into the kitchen where Jamie lit a lamp. His mother, a tall thin woman, joined them there, her long dark hair flowing in her movement.

"What's happened?" she asked.

"Dunno," her husband answered. "Jest found him at the door."

"Where's he hurt?" Katherine wondered as she prodded the dog in search of his wounds.

"He's not," Jonathan observed, his face twisted by a sudden horrible thought. "Oh my God!" he exclaimed. "It's the family!"

"What?" his wife didn't follow.

"Raiders?" Jamie whispered the question, afraid of the answer.

"Yes," his father confirmed. "Jamie, git Doc Porter. Tell him ta meet me here soon's he kin, thet we're goin ta the Kinkade place. I'll saddle the horses. Katherine, go over ta the saloon an wake Charley. Tell him what's up 'n ta git some riders an meet me at the Kinkade's."

Jamie ran off in his nightshirt to find the doctor. The girls, awakened by the flurry of activity, joined their parents to find out what was happening. Pounder was left in their care while the marshall and his wife quickly dressed and prepared to depart. Jonathan brought the horses around as Jamie returned to report that the doctor was on his way.

"Kin I come?" the boy asked.

"Not now," the man replied. "Wait here an look ta the dog while we first find out what's out there."

Jamie accepted his father's decision, wanting very much to know what had happened, yet knowing it could be dangerous. Doc Porter arrived on horseback, his medical supplies stowed in his saddlebags. Mrs. Fowler had returned to report that Charley would be along within the hour with as much help as he could find.

The night was at its blackest—in the last hour before dawn would begin to lighten the eastern horizon. The three riders were ready to depart. Pounder barked wildly, protesting at being left behind. The door closed behind them as Doc and the Fowlers mounted their horses and headed at a gallop out the familiar country road.

Dawn had brightened the morning horizon as clattering hooves crossed the bridge and entered the killing ground. The three reined their horses to a stop at the corner of the dwelling and gazed horror-stricken at the scene before them.

"Oh, dear God," the woman gasped.

They quickly dismounted and hurried to the boy and his mother. Doc knew at a glance that Laura was dead. He turned his attention to the boy as Mrs. Fowler knelt by the woman and her husband stood with the horses, studying the death and destruction, trying to comprehend why a man could be so heartless.

Daryll Porter was an experienced doctor on the downhill end of his fifties. Straight black hair had an abundant mix of white. He was a large man, over six feet in height, and still physically trim from constant activity in a demanding practice. On his knees beside the still figure, he gently searched for an indication of life. The boy's skin was warm to the touch, but pale from loss of blood. A faint pulse was evident on the side of his neck.

"Dee's alive," Doc reported as he continued to search gently to find the extent of his wounds.

"Laura's dead," Mrs. Fowler stated as she caressed the side of her friend's face. The tears came and she could not hold them back.

"I guessed as much," Doc observed. "What about the others, Jon?"

The marshall turned to check on the two who lay in the yard. After shoving at each body with a toe, he replied, "They're both quite dead, Doc. An even if they weren't, I'd 'ave finished 'em." There was bitterness in his voice. He returned to stand by the doctor. "How bad?" he asked.

"I'm not sure." He looked up at the woman. "Kate, could ya see if the table is clear inside so Jon 'n me kin bring the boy in?"

Mrs. Fowler stood, still staring at the dead woman. She forced herself to turn away and to enter the house.

"Take his feet, Jon, an try ta keep him flat out."

The two men carefully slipped their arms under the small, still form and eased him from the ground. They carried him inside and placed him on the wooden surface of the table. Katherine took the water bucket from the floor near the drain board and left to refill it with fresh water. Doc Porter began to work on his young patient while the marshall went out to fetch his medical supplies.

The boy's shirt was cut away and the pieces tossed to the floor. An ominous hole was found beneath the fabric and crusting blood. Torn flesh was embedded with fragments of bone and shredded muscle tissue.

"Looks real bad," the marshall observed as he stood by to help.

"It surely is," Doc agreed. "But luck may be on the boy's side." He continued to look further in search of wounds.

"How d' ya mean?" the woman asked as she poured some water into a basin.

"It don't look like there's damage inside." His examination finished, he looked up to give instructions. "Jon, find a sheet and rip it inta bandage strips. Kate, ya help me here."

As the two worked over the boy and the marshall prepared bandages, riders arrived in the yard. Mr. Fowler finished ripping down the sheet before stepping out to organize a pursuit. The boy was bathed and the wound was cleaned out. Chips of bone, dirt, and pieces of fabric were picked from the torn tissue. The bullet had ripped between two ribs, shattering bone and tearing flesh. One rib was splintered, another broken, and two more were cracked.

The marshall returned. "Ramsey 'n Jensen 'r stayin on ta take care a thin's outside," he reported. "Charley 'n me 'r takin the rest ta see if we kin track the skunks 'n clean 'em out. See ya when we git back." He was gone.

Galloping hoofbeats faded as Doc and Kate continued their work.

"What's important," Porter explained as they worked, "is thet these ribs not be moved til they heal. Otherwise they kin rupture a lung. Then it's all over." New bleeding continued as he worked and had to be constantly sponged out with a cloth. "Hold this fer me while I find my sewin thin's."

A packet of sinew thread and sewing needles was taken from the bag and one of the needles was prepared with a length of the line. The open flesh was pulled together to cover the wound, then carefully sewn shut. Some bleeding continued to seep around the stitching. The work was covered with a dressing. All was wrapped tightly with bandage strips and tied securely to help hold the wound closed and to keep the ribs in place.

The head wound was a deep trench, cut through the scalp, high on the left side. It, too, was cleaned, stitched, and wrapped. Scraps of board were brought in from the barnyard fence and placed between the mattress and rope spring on the boy's bed to firm it up and protect the ribs. When the bed had been prepared and the boy had been dressed in a clean pair of johns, he was carefully moved to his room for the long vigil of care and healing that would follow.

Outside, the two men who had remained had righted the wagon which had survived the fire, brought in the horses, and rigged temporary harnessing with the rope which they cut from the gate. The dead woman's body had been wrapped in a flannel sheet and placed in the wagon. The others had been loaded and covered with a blanket. Mrs. Fowler had bundled up some of Laura's clothing to send along for burial garments. The two left with instructions to ask Sally Riggs to come out and bring the younger Fowler children. Laureen, the eldest, could stay to look after the needs of the boarding house if she needed.

The wagon rattled out of the yard toward town. Doc and Kate cleaned up the operating theater and returned it to use as a kitchen once more. The medical bag was packed and set aside on a pantry shelf. Then the woman began to prepare a pot of soup while the man started a fire in the stove and prepared another in the fireplace should it be needed in the evening.

Duane lay unconscious. He had not moved in the course of the surgery nor stirred since he had been tucked into bed. The pale face rested on the clean pillow. White bandages about his head had reddened at the wound with new bleeding. The quilt covering showed an almost imperceptible rise and fall of slow, shallow breathing. The eyes closed, the face without expression; the small body lay committed to the course of time and healing, in the care of friends who loved him.

By the end of the day, Mrs. Riggs, the children, and the dog arrived at the farm. Pounder went directly to the bedroom to find his master, as all who were present checked in on his condition. The dog whined, beseeching the boy to acknowledge him. Doc assured the dog that he would be all right and patted him gently on the head. Pounder sat down by the chair to watch until all had left the room. Then he settled on the floor across the door and began his vigil.

It was decided that Mrs. Riggs would stay on and care for Duane. Her husband was also away to the war and the boarding house had few patrons. Jamie could stay and help with chores and as needed. The wagon had been outfitted with harness and tack from the livery stable. It would be kept beside the house and the gear stored under canvass in the wagon bed. The team and livestock could forage in the meadows. Mrs. Fowler and her daughter would go home. She and the two girls would take turns tending to needs at the boarding house and at the Fowler house. Doc Porter and the marshall would check in periodically. As soon as Duane was strong enough, he would be moved into a room at the boarding house and live with Mrs. Riggs. The Kinkade house would be closed up until such time as Andrew returned from the war and could take charge of his family's affairs.

All except Jamie and Mrs. Riggs departed the following morning. They kept their vigil in the days that followed—changing the bandages each day and trying to force some broth or tea between stilled lips so that the boy's strength could be maintained and some nourishment might help the healing. Attempts to feed the dog or to get him to move were fruitless. He drank some water and occasionally nibbled a scrap of food, but otherwise remained in his place near his friend.

Infection set in by the second day and damp cloths wrung from a basin of cold water were used to fight a stubborn fever. Duane began to stir as his condition worsened and he became delirious.

Jamie and Mrs. Riggs took turns staying by his side around the clock during the crisis. Continual feeding of broth and tea helped to keep the boy from weakening. After two frightening days, the puss cleared from the wound, the fever broke, and the boy calmed. He settled into a relaxed sleep which lasted another day and a half.

Finally, nearly a week following that day of fire, Duane began to waken. Pounder barked joyously and bathed his master's face with his tongue. The woman quickly put an end to such behavior as she and Jamie rejoiced in the boy's recovery. There were tears of joy followed by a time of grief as Duane recalled what had happened. He was told of his mother's burial in the church yard shortly after the killing and of what was known about the raiders—the two he and Pounder had killed and the failed attempt to track them down. He in turn related the story of what had taken place that day.

The pace of his heeling quickened. But it was the end of the second week before he was permitted out of bed. Several more days passed before he could remain up any length of time. During that week the bandages came off the head wound and the stitching was cut away and removed from his skin. The outside had healed, but the ribs had a ways to go. They were to be kept wrapped for at least three more weeks.

Late in the third week, it was decided that Duane was strong enough for the move to town. The house was closed up and all personal possessions were packed and loaded into the wagon, including the boy's bed. Doc came out to tend the boy on the move and to be sure he could safely stand the trip. Duane was assisted into the wagon and settled into his bed where he was to remain on his back during the course of the journey. He found it extremely painful and spent much of his effort fighting tears The dog sat in the wagon bed beside him and the doctor rode seated on a trunk by the bed. Their presence was a comfort.

The trip was long and arduous. By the time they arrived at Riggs's Boarding House, Duane was exhausted. He was moved into a back room above the kitchen. The bed had been freshly made and the room cleaned for his coming. Doc Porter carried the boy up the back steps from the kitchen and helped him change into his night shirt. Pounder stayed close by and followed every detail of settling in. Duane was tucked into bed and a light meal of thin soup and a glass of milk was carried up on a tray. He ate slowly while Jamie brought his clothing and personal things to be stowed in the wardrobe. The bed was taken apart and stored in the barn. The wagon and team were turned over to the livery stable for care.

It had been a hard day. When all had finally left the room, the dog went to the bed to check on his friend. He nuzzled the hand that lay on the bed covers and was rewarded by a gentle stroking of his nose and a weak good night. Pounder settled on the floor across the door. Duane lay staring out the window at the sky beyond. Quiet tears of loss and loneliness slid down his cheeks. He closed his eyes and allowed exhaustion to take over as he drifted into dreamless sleep.

*　　*　　*

It was early the following morning. Duane had finished his breakfast which Mrs. Riggs had brought up on a tray. Pounder had been a great help as he ate half the food. The boy really wasn't very hungry. He settled back against the pillow, too weak to lift the tray from his lap to the bedside table. The dog settled on the floor beside the bed. He was busy getting up the last crumbs from the floor. The boy had closed his eyes and was drifting off to sleep. Light footsteps bounced up the back steps and down the hall to the bedroom. Duane opened his eyes to find Jamie standing in the door.

"Ya awake?" his friend asked.

"Yea," Duane replied. "Could ya move this tray fer me?"

"Sure," The dog looked up as Jamie entered the room. "Pa sent these letters fer ya." He handed them to the patient as he lifted the tray to the table. "They're from yer Pa. Been here a while, but ya bin too sick."

Jamie settled in a small wooden rocker with upholstered seat and back panels, while Duane stared at the letters. Tears came to his eyes without warning and slid down his cheeks. The writings were addressed to his ma and him. The younger boy swallowed hard to force a painful lump from his throat. Pounder wandered over to sit beside the rocker and pushed his muzzle under an idle hand.

"Hi, fella," Jamie greeted hoarsely. "Ya want some attention, huh."

The dog woofed softly and the boy stroked the massive head. Pounder rested his chin on Jamie's knee and enjoyed the attention. Duane finally wiped his eyes with his shirt sleeve and opened the letters. He read silently for several minutes while Jamie attended to Pounder.

"Eny news?" Jamie asked as Duane let his hand fall and rested the letters on the bedcovers.

"Pa's bin assigned ta the 13th Arkansas under a Colonel James Tappan. They're s'posed ta be on the way ta places along the Mississippi. He's not sure where. There's bin some sickness in camp. He's a corporal now. Last month there was a battle north a here in Springfield, Missouri. Thet's 'bout it."

"Who won the battle?"

The dog's eyes followed the speakers.

"We did." He carefully folded the letters and slipped them under his pillow. "I'll read em agin later," Duane explained. He turned his eyes to his friend. "What's gonna happen ta the farm? This is September already. It's time ta harvest."

"Pa'll take care a thin's. He's already talkin ta friends 'bout goin out next week ta git the crops in."

Duane closed his eyes. For a moment, no more was said. A tear slipped free. His lips quivered. When he opened his eyes, they were wet. His voice cracked as he spoke. "It jest don't seem real."

"Hey," Jamie broke in. "Ya need yer rest." As he stood, so did the dog. "I'll take this tray down 'n stop back near mid day." Jamie reached for the tray.

"Okay," Duane smiled weakly. "See ya then."

Pounder followed the boy to the door. There he settled on the floor as Jamie waved to his friend and departed. Duane reached under the pillow for the letters and read through the first a second time. He was tired, emotionally worn out. Resting the letters at his side, he closed his eyes and slipped into a tired slumber.

*   *   *

Summer drifted into Fall. Mrs. Riggs and Jamie were Duane's constant companions. She tended him as his mother would have, but as a friend. Jamie became like a brother. As the days passed, the recovery progressed and the boy was able to spend some minutes, then hours, in the rocking chair. Finally, he could move about the house and enjoy spending hours in the kitchen where he could be closer to the day's activity. He wrote to his father to tell him of the raid and his mother's death. The boys would visit for hours; then, when Duane was able to sit up, play at checkers or cards. On some days Jamie brought a copy of the newspaper and they would spread it across the kitchen table to read the news of the war. As his strength improved, Duane helped Mrs. Riggs about the kitchen. Pounder had claimed an approved spot in the corner near the back stairway. He was not permitted in the rest of the dwelling as long as there were boarders. He did, however, consent to taking walks with Jamie while Duane remained behind in the kitchen.

In the weeks that followed, Duane was permitted to leave the house for short walks. The boys wandered to the Marshall's Office, the newspaper office, for a walk about the streets, or down by the river. Some days, when their friends were out swimming, Duane would sit on the bank and Jamie would join the others in the water. Rainy days were usually spent in the comfort of the boarding house kitchen.

The leaves turned. The days shortened. The weather became grey and chilled. Autumn advanced toward Winter. Late September saw action to the north in Lexington, Missouri. As October passed, so, too, did Duane's eleventh birthday. It was a day of particular loneliness. No one knew of its significance. Those who did—those who mattered—were absent. The boy kept its importance to himself. Early November saw battle at Belmont, Missouri, across the Mississippi from Columbus, Kentucky. According to his pa's last letter, the 13th was to be in that area as part of a buildup of fortifications into western Kentucky.

*　*　*

The snow fell softly and silently that Christmas. Duane stood gazing out the window into the woodlot and watched as it thickened on the tree limbs, fence rails, and firewood. A speck of red flitted along a fence post, then onto wood chips in the yard. The cardinal looked for the bread crumbs Mrs. Riggs had thrown out that morning.

The smells and sounds of Christmas dinner being prepared trespassed on his thoughts, and he felt a sudden sense of sadness. This was his first Christmas alone.

"I'm goin afta wood fer the stove," Duane called as he grabbed his coat. He dashed out the door without waiting for an answer. Pounder followed at his heels.

The boy paused on the back porch so as not to frighten the bird, and ordered the dog to sit quietly. He tried to concentrate on the movement of red and the falling snow and to push his sadness out of his mind. The cardinal flew off into a tree and chirped brightly at the boy. Then the thoughts and memories flooded back into his mind and overwhelmed him. Duane sat on the snowy steps and sobbed quietly. The dog rested a consoling chin on the boy's leg.

"Why, God! Why did it haf ta be! Why? Why?"

Mrs. Riggs turned from the stove and sensed the boy's sadness. She checked out the window and saw him, lonely and crying, huddled on the back steps, his dog close at his side, with snow crusting on his clothes and the animal's back. She opened the door and called softly.

"Dee, git yerself 'n yer dog in here afor ya ketch yer death. Come in an git warm." There was a soft understanding for his sadness in her voice.

The boy rose from the steps, went into the warm kitchen and the waiting arms of the landlady. Pounder followed to his corner near the stairway and sat, watching the boy. The two stood there a long moment, the boy crying out his anguish, and the kind woman wishing she could comfort him.

*　*　*

There were no letters and little news through the winter. Much of the army had gone into a long camp. It was an afternoon in late February when Mrs. Riggs called from the back door.

"Dee!" her voice carried in the chill air. "There's a letter here fer ya from somewhere in Mississippi. Jamie thinks it's from yer pa."

Duane, who had been gathering wood for the supper cooking, dropped everything and raced for the kitchen door in his hurried excitement to read the letter. Pounder looked up from his corner, awakened from his nap by the banging door.

"Where?" he asked breathlessly.

"It's right here. Slow down fer ya hurt yerself."

Snatching the letter from her hand, he grabbed a bread knife and tore open the cover paper.

"Dee!" But she decided not to say anything more.

Not bothering to remove his coat, the boy fell into a chair and spread his letter on the table.

February 2, 1862

My dearest Laura and Dee,

I'm sorry I didn't get to write since November last. Federal troops under General Grant attacked our camps at Belmont, Missouri. The fighting was fierce and involved Yankee gunboats, artillery, infantry. Losses were heavy, but we finally drove them off. I got a battlefield promotion to sergeant.

I received your letter of July, but any that may have followed haven't reached me yet. Were you able to get the crops in all right and do you have enough for the winter? Did you have a good Christmas and holiday season? I missed you both very much.

There's been a lot of sickness through the camp. I was laid up about three weeks. Things seem to be going all right here. We're a little short on everything but we're making do.

We're going on to Tennessee. That same Yankee general, Grant, has been making things hot up there. His forces have been threatening Fort Henry. We're going in to lend support.

I love you both very much and sure do miss you. Sure hope this war is over soon.

Your devoted husband and father,
Andrew Kinkade
Sergeant, 13th Arkansas

PS—Laura, the socks got holes in the holes now. We're hoping to pick off a Union supply train on our way and get us some new clothes.

Duane looked at the letter a long time. His eyes began to burn and an uncontrollable tear fell onto the paper. Mrs. Riggs noticed the sudden quiet and hurt that enveloped the boy as he read his letter.

"Is som'thin wrong, Dee?" she ventured.

"He don't know," he answered without turning. "He neve got my letter! He ain't knowin Ma's dead!" Duane turned to her and she saw the awful hurt in his eyes.

Carefully he folded the letter and tucked it into his shirt. He wiped a shirt sleeve across his eyes.

"I best git thet wood now," he said listlessly and shuffled out the door.

Mrs. Riggs watched him from the window as the gusty grey wind whipped about him. The dog lowered his head to his paws and watched for the boy's return. Slowly and deliberately, Duane picked up each piece of wood and placed it in his left arm. Leaving the shelter of the shed, he again crossed the grey world of wind that was the back yard of the boarding house and entered into the warmth of the kitchen. Dumping the wood in its box, he hung his coat on its peg by the door.

"I'm goin ta my room fer a while."

"I'll call ya when supper's on," Mrs. Riggs acknowledged softly.

She turned to the table to finish preparing the meat for the oven. As Duane mounted the kitchen stairway, went to his room and closed the door, the dog followed. Inside the room, Pounder settled in his corner and watched his young master.

Kicking his boots under the chair, the boy flopped down on his stomach across the bed with his feet dangling over one side and his hands and head over the other. He stared at the floor and his eyes followed the cracks in the floorboards until they blurred into the same daze of nothingness that his mind was in. Everything was nothing. He felt like an ant looking down at the floor from miles away.

Duane forced his eyes to focus, bringing him back to reality. Rolling over on his back he looked up toward the ceiling. It, too, seemed to back away from him and again he felt small and inconspicuous. Time became eternity and he lay there for a long time in a state of nothingness. Gradually he again began to think.

He reached into his shirt and withdrew the letter. Slowly opening it up, he gazed at the lines. A sudden urge took hold of him—an urge to find his father. It surged throughout his body giving him new energy and filling him with excitement. The ceiling no longer looked so high nor the floor so far down.

He looked at the letter again. "We're on our way to Tennessee . . . Fort Henry."

Suddenly Duane knew just exactly what he was going to do. A military wagon train expected through day after tomorrow was probably headed for Ozark. If he could sneak into one of the wagons and get to Ozark, he would try to find William Kearney, captain of the sternwheeler, Ozark Queen, whom he knew from earlier visits with his pa. Maybe he could get the captain to take him along on his next trip down the Arkansas and on south to Vicksburg. Once there, he might be able to get in with a unit headed north.

The dog sensed the boy's excitement. Pounding his tail on the floor, he shared his enthusiasm as he followed the preparations with his eyes.

Taking two blankets from the drawer in the wardrobe, Duane rolled a change of clothes into them and tied the bundle tightly together. This he tucked carefully into a corner of the cabinet so that it would be ready when the chance came for him to leave. He thought a minute as to what to do about food. Some leftovers wrapped in a paper would solve the problem. He lay down again and in his mind he saw his trip and imagined how it would be when he found his pa in Tennessee.

The boy passed the remainder of the afternoon in his dream world until it was shattered by the woman's voice calling him to supper. Snapping back to the present, Duane grabbed his boots from under the chair and stuffed his feet into them. He and the dog were out the door and halfway to the stairs when he remembered the letter. Rushing back to the room, he carefully refolded it, then placed it in the rope holding his bundle together, while Pounder stood waiting in the doorway.

"Comb yer hair, an wash yer hands," Mrs. Riggs ordered when Duane bounced down the stairs and into the kitchen. "An I'd appreciate it if ya'd bring the rolls with ya when ya come ta the table." Her tone was kinder.

The rest sure did him good, she thought as she carried the tray of vegetables into the dining room. Pounder settled in his corner to enjoy his dish of table scraps.

"Taylor," Mrs. Riggs asked a long-term boarder as she set things on the table, "would ya do me the honors a carvin tanight?"

"Of course, Sally. Have ya heard eny news from Joseph?"

"Not since last month. But Dee got a letter taday from his pa."

"Someone call?" Duane asked entering with the rolls.

"What did ya hear from yer pa?" the man asked.

The boy set the rolls on the table by Mrs. Riggs, then took his seat partway down the side. "Pa's letter was a might slow ta gittin here. He sent it the beginnin a the month. But he says Gen'ral Grant's afta Fort Henry 'n thet he's afta Gen'ral Grant. He also said his socks got holes in the holes . . ."

A burst of laughter followed, interrupting after the last comment.

" . . . 'n thet they plan ta git new clothes off'n the first Yankee supply train they come across."

"Reverend, will ya ask the blessin," the landlady requested. They bowed their heads in silence.

"Father God, look down on us as we are gathered here to partake of this food. Bless those who are absent from our midst and bring them safely home. Amen."

The room filled with conversation—each told of his day's events and they discussed the war.

The reverend, who always ate supper at the boarding house, spoke up. "Sally, ya set a mighty fine meal."

"Reverend, ya always say thet an I thank ya fer the compliment."

"Mr. Andrews," she turned to one of the guests, "I understand yer leavin us tamorra. We sure enjoyed yer stayin here."

"I rather enjoyed it maself," he commented. "I'll always know were ta stay wheneve I'm in these parts agin."

"Boy, ya said yer pa was headed fer Tennessee?" another guest asked. "Do ya know what part a Tennessee he's headed fer?"

"No sir," Duane replied. "He jest said Tennessee."

"Did he way where'bouts in Mississippi he was 'r what unit he was with?"

"He didn't say enythin 'bout thet at all. The letter was posted from Mississippi."

"Hol on a minute," Taylor cut in. "Ya got an awful lot a questions, mister. Unhealthy questions at thet. Why the sudden inter'st in the boy's pa?"

"Jest curious."

"Well ya keep yer curiosity ta yerself. We don't care ta discuss the where'bouts of ar relatives with strangers."

As conversation shifted and the minutes passed, Duane sensed that this stranger was staring at him. The man was well dressed. Yet it occurred to the boy that there was something familiar about him. By meal's end, he had become very uncomfortable and wanted to get away quickly.

Back in the kitchen he asked, "Is it all right ta go ta Jamie's fer a bit? Me 'n Pounder need ta git out some."

"Sure, Dee," the woman smiled. "Don't be long."

He took down his coat and hat and wrapped a scarf to tie the hat against the wind. Mrs. Riggs left the room to bring more leftovers from the table while the boy and his dog headed through the hall toward the front door. As they stepped out into the storm and headed for the Fowler house, he sensed that someone was following. They were nearing the Marshall's Office when Pounder suddenly stopped. An ominous growl rumbled deep in his throat.

The dog turned, muscles taught, ready to break into a run. Duane restrained him as he turned to see what caused such behavior. The stranger stood, ghostlike in the swirling snow, a revolver in his hand. Pounder erupted into a frenzy of barking and struggled to break free. As the stranger leveled the gun's barrel at the dog and pulled back the hammer, the boy knew and released the fury of the dog. This was one of the raiders and he had recognized the boy.

Gunshots roared—two, so close together to seem as one. The man flew backwards, sprawling in the snow as the mighty dog yelped and collapsed in mid-flight. Crimson red splattered the snow where the stranger fell, and puddled out from the great furry form which lay still near the boy.

"Nooo!" he cried as he fell in the snow beside his friend.

Footsteps approached from behind. He glanced up to see Marshall Fowler approaching, gun drawn, smoke wisping from the barrel. The boy buried his face in the warm fur of the strong neck. Uncontrolled sobbing wracked the small body as he wept bitterly and his insides felt wretched with pain and grief. The marshall checked the stranger, then holstered his gun. He returned to kneel beside the boy.

A small crowd began to gather. Mrs. Riggs spotted the boy on the street and came running.

"Oh, no!" she shrieked. "Not Dee!"

Jonathan stood and caught her. "It aint the boy, Sally. It's his dog."

"Oh, God!" she cried. "Why must you hurt him so." The man sought to comfort her as she wept on his shoulder.

Someone had gone for the doctor and he approached the subdued crowd. A few began to turn away. He saw the boy on the ground, the dog, the blood. Doc Porter knelt beside them and put an arm across the boy's shoulder.

"Dee, let me git a look," he spoke softly. The sobbing boy shook his head. "Come on," the man pleaded. "I can't help if ya don't let me have a look."

He eased the boy off the dog.

"Ow!" Duane cried as he grabbed his chest and collapsed in the snow.

"Quick, Jon!" the doctor caught the boy in his arms, "help me get him into yer office." As they lifted him from the ground he continued. "Sally, cover thet dog 'n keep him warm till I git back."

A spectator offered a coat and the woman knelt by the dog while Duane was carried to the warmth of the building. He was carefully eased onto the desk. Wincing with pain, he heaved a long sigh of relief once he was down. The tears continued.

"I'm okay, Doc," he sobbed. "It jest hurts ta move." Again the tears overflowed. "Why did he hafta kill Pounder?"

"We don't know thet he did," the doctor spoke softly. "Ya stay here with the marshall while I go see."

The two men exchanged nods of understanding as the one left and the other remained with the boy. After what seemed forever, Mrs. Riggs opened the door and entered the warmth of the room.

There were tears in her eyes and joy on her face. "Yer dog's alive, Dee!" she beamed. "They're takin him ta Doc's office 'n ya kin see him there in a hour."

Disbelief and joy lit the boy's face. Tears came with the smile and broken sobs of emotional relief as the woman embraced him to reassure him that all would be well. Even Jonathan's eyes glistened wet as he spoke.

"Sally, ya take the boy home 'n mind he don't strain his self any more. After he's warmed up, ya go ta Doc's, he'll wanta check him out, too." The marshall helped the boy to his feet. "I'll tend thin's here."

The boy moved slowly to avoid the pain in his chest as the two moved toward the door. When they had gone, Marshall Fowler reached his coat and hat from their pegs, then he, too, departed to attend to the stranger in the street.

* * *

It had been Duane's intention to tell Jamie of his plans that stormy night and to arrange for him to keep Pounder during his absence. As it turned out, he never spoke to his friend. Pounder's wound was serious but not likely to be fatal. He had been shot through the neck, suffering torn muscle tissue and loss of blood.

Duane had strained the area of his injury—pulling tissue and bone, but without serious damage. It would be painful for several days.

Pounder was very weak when the boy saw him that night. He whined painfully and tried to lick the boy's hand. The dog was unable to lift his head or move his body. A bandage was wrapped about his neck and he lay motionless on his side. Tears of joy slid down the boy's face as he knelt beside his friend and gently caressed his head.

In bed that night he pondered the wisdom of his earlier decision. Pounder needed him now. The next day was spent with the dog at Doc Porter's office. Pounder slept for much of the time, but as he had kept his vigil by the boy, so now the boy kept his vigil by his dog. Jamie joined him and he learned that the military train had been delayed by the storm. Duane decided not to tell the other boy of his plan but to wait and see how his dog recovered.

Within a few days, Pounder was strong enough to move home again. A comfortable place was prepared in the corner of the kitchen and there he was to stay during the balance of his recovery. The bedroom felt empty without the dog's presence in his corner, and Duane lay awake at night thinking of Pounder and contemplating his decision.

The military wagons passed through a week late. Duane decided to go. His dog was much stronger and could get along without him.

*   *   *

Duane excused himself from breakfast to take some table scraps to the dog. While everyone else lingered in the dining room, the boy set a plate of scraps for the dog, then searched for some leftovers for himself. The pantry contained a piece of cooked beef from the previous night, and a tray on the table contained some extra biscuits from breakfast. A piece of wrapping paper was taken from a storage drawer and an empty flour sack from a closet shelf.

Duane wrapped the food and packed it in the sack, then set it out on the back porch.

Making a hurried trip to his room, he returned with the bundle, checking to see if the kitchen was empty before he slipped across the room and out the back door. Grabbing the food pack en route, he crossed to the wood shed where he stowed his gear in preparation for his departure. To make it look good, he returned with an armful of wood. But no one was in the kitchen.

Returning once more to his room, the boy took paper and pencil and wrote a note for Mrs. Riggs. He told her he had gone to find his pa and asked if she could take care of Pounder. If that wasn't possible, Jamie would probably do it. He folded the paper to lay it down, but paused as he remembered something else. Writing once more, he added his thanks for all she had done and closed it with his love. The note was left on the pillow. It was time to go.

Duane returned to the kitchen and settled on his knees beside his dog. "Pounder, I'm goin away. Ya gotta stay here 'n be real good. Ya gotta git well, too, 'n be strong fer when I git back. I dunno how long I'll be gone, but I am comin back." He hugged the furry bulk gently so as not to hurt his wound, then kissed him on his muzzle. "I love ya, Pounder," he whispered as the tears slid down his face. The dog licked at the salty drops as he returned his love for the boy. "I'm gonna miss ya som'thin fierce." Another tear escaped and he quickly wiped it away.

Duane stood slowly. As he reached down his coat and hat, he looked once more at Pounder. Their eyes met. Sudden emotion rushed through the boy. His eyes blurred and his throat tightened thick and painful. He wanted so much to cry. Pounder knew. It showed in his eyes. He had to go now or he wouldn't be able to make himself do it.

It was clear outside. After slipping on the coat and cramming his hat on his head, Duane stuffed his scarf and a pair of gloves into his pockets. He turned to the back door.

"I'm goin ta Jamie's," he called as he hurried out the door and pulled it shut before Mrs. Riggs could respond.

Once outside, Duane went directly to the wood shed, gathered his gear, then headed toward the livery barn where the wagons had been gathered. It was still too early for people to be about or businesses to open. Even so, the boy followed the back alleys to avoid being seen and approached the livery from behind the corral fencing.

Activity was concentrated around two wagons which were being loaded with extra sacks of grain. The teams had already been hitched and stood ready to depart. Several supply wagons, parked alongside the barn, were temporarily unattended. Duane chose one of these, worked his way along the fencing, and approached the back end of the wagon. The bed was filled with crates of stores and supplies, and covered over with a canvass. The boy lifted a corner of the cover in search of open space within. He safely swung his gear over the tail of the wagon and dropped it into a narrow slot between the sideboards and a crate. With his hands free, he pushed at barrels and boxes until he was able to create a space large enough to crawl into. Voices approached from in front of the barn.

"Sergeant Winters," someone called. "Git yer men ta their wagons and prepare ta move out."

"Yes, sir," a gruff voice responded.

Grabbing the tail boards with both hands, Duane shoved off from the ground and hauled himself over the edge. Squirming down into the tight space he had created, the boy pushed the cover back over the end boards.

The wagon rocked sideways as the troopers climbed to the seat. There was an organized commotion as the troops were assembled and preparations were completed to move out. It seemed an hour, but it was only a matter of minutes before the orders ran down the line and the train of wagons began to move.

For a moment Duane felt a strong urge to abandon his plan. He loved Pounder and hated to leave him. There was Jamie's close friendship. He knew Mrs. Riggs would worry and he didn't want to hurt her. He did love her and knew she loved him. But he missed his pa. He wanted so much to be with him and to feel secure in his presence. The pangs of indecision hurt.

The wagon lurched into motion and rocked him against a crate. It was too late now. He was on his way. He was committed.

Suddenly he felt very lonely.

EPILOGUE

It was getting on toward dark when the wagon finally ceased its bumpy monotony. The day was wintry cold, yet beads of sweat dampened the boy's whole body as he fought the pain in his chest, aggravated by the long and rough ride. Duane grew tense and listened cautiously as orders passed among the troops to pull the wagons together for the night.

"Sergeant Winters, take yer wagon under the trees there 'long with the rest a the supply wagons." The slow movement of the officer's horse could be heard as the voice traveled up the road. "Sergeant Reilly, set the company street 'long the east side a the road." The orders grew faint as the lieutenant rode back to the front of the column.

One more short ride and the wagon came to a final rest.

"Hey, Kelly! Gimme a hand with these horses," the driver called.

Duane watched for his chance to crawl out of the wagon unnoticed. Looking out from under the canvass, he could see in the dim evening light, the organized commotion as the camp was established. He heard the jingle of trace chains and the clatter of cross-trees as the team was unhitched and the wagon's tongue was allowed to drop to the ground with a thunk. Everyone was occupied, either with the placement of the wagons or the setup of tent canvass.

With painful slowness Duane worked himself free of his cramped quarters. He managed to crawl up and lay along top the tailboards where he was able to drag his gear up and over their edge. Dropping his bedroll to the ground below, he rolled off the hard rail and let himself fall to the grass. There he collapsed to hands and knees to grit his teeth and allow the pain to subside before moving further. He pondered how he was going to leave the camp without being caught. The boy collected his gear and stood up, keeping close to the darkness of the wagon and its shadows.

He shook within as an authoritative voice startled him from behind. "Boy, what ya think yer doin here?" But before Duane could respond, "Go on 'n run 'long now. This ain't no kid's playin place." Without further comment, the soldier disappeared into the routine of the camp.

Glancing about him, Duane took his bearings and found himself on the outskirts of Ozark. The town itself was a few hundred yards beyond the worm fence that struck out perpendicular to the road, just ahead of the wagon. The boy carefully eased his gear over a shoulder. Then circling around the horse lines, Duane turned in the direction of town. Following the edge of the field near the roadside, he walked along slowly, keeping to the tree shadows and trying to conserve his energy. Already exhausted from the ride and the pain, he held to the knowledge that the riverboat docking area was less than a mile ahead. Hopefully the Ozark Queen would be there and Captain Kearney would still be her skipper.

"Sergeant!" The boy overheard the conversation as he passed the edge of the tent street. "Lieutenant Reynolds will take charge."

"Yes, Sir," the man acknowledged.

The captain continued. "I'm on my way ta see the rive'boat is ready ta take us on come mornin. Ya help the lieutenant by seein the cook wagon is open 'n runnin supper. I 'spect ta be back near seven."

The two exchanged sharp salutes, then the captain wheeled his horse and galloped toward the town. Duane moved on, satisfied to know that the riverboat was to be there.

*   *   *

Dimly lit windows cast an eerie glow and a multitude of mysterious shadows about the streets along the waterfront. There was a great deal of pedestrian activity in the early evening hours as stevedores and sailors wandered from one bar or card game to another, or gathered in small knots to pass the latest gossip before drifting on to some rented room for the night. Apart from the movement of nightlife in the streets, the boat landing wharfs were a silent maze of freight and shipping goods, some having recently arrived and some waiting to be loaded aboard a freight or packet boat. Many small skiffs and sailing boats bobbed in the water near the landing. The only large vessel was tied up port side to the freight wharf. It was the stern-wheeler, Ozark Queen.

A few lamps were lit on each of her decks along the outer cabin walls nearest the forward stairs and ladders. Illumination glowed through the windows of the engine room, the pilot house, a few cabins, and crew's quarters. No activity was evident on board since most of the crew had gone ashore for the evening. The river's water lapped gently under the boat's bow and against its stilled paddles. A murmur of distant and indistinct voices hung on the evening air, highlighted by an occasional raucous outburst of laughter or profanity. Otherwise, the waterfront was quiet. A horse snorted its boredom. The single steed was tied to a post near the gangplank to the boat. In the shadows of the main deck, two men were absorbed in animated conversation, their whispers barely audible to a quiet observer.

Duane watched from his hiding place perched on a flour barrel on the shadow side of a wall of crates. He had approached the vessel under cover of the waterfront clutter and had seen the captain's horse tied at the gangway. Thinking it best to await the officer's departure, the boy had crept as close as he dared to try and overhear the conversation. He had also confirmed for himself that this was the Queen and the other man with the captain was the boat's skipper, William Kearney. While Duane waited on the barrel, he nibbled on the beef and biscuits in the flour sack.

Captain Kearney was a slender figure, just shy of six feet in height. He cut a crisp appearance in his tailored blue uniform and short-billed cap with polished black visor. Long sideburns and a neatly trimmed mustache added an authoritative dignity to his character.

"No, Captain," Kearney was saying, "I'm glad ta help anytime." The voices rose and fell on the chilled evening breeze, and the aroma of his pipe smoke scented the night air. "Now to your men. They won't have it easy by any means. Ya say ya've seventy-five?"

"Yea, an' nearly a dozen supply wagons 'n twenty-eight horses." The two turned toward the ship's bow.

"Thet'll make thin's awfully crowded," remarked Kearney. "They'll have all this deck. But as ya see, much a the inner space is taken by the engine boilers 'n gear drive. There's storage 'n some cabin space up front. But once ya put yer wagons on the side decks 'n yer horses in the storeroom spaces, ya'll not have much space left. Yer enlisted men stay to the main deck. Yer officers kin use cabins aft on the passenger deck. We do have some passengers in the forward cabins. We also haf ta pick up a small company a soldiers an supplies at Pine Bluff." They arrived at the main staircase and started up. "Let's go up an I'll show ya what's fer yer use."

"Fine," the Confederate officer replied. Captain Masters was an experienced soldier, tall, clean-shaven, and busy fidgeting with a handful of papers. Folding the papers into one hand, he continued as the two reached the top step, "We'll come aboard afta daybreak. Thet way we'll have good light ta put up the horses an git the wagons on board."

The two men became lost to the boy in the silence of the vessel's shadows. Duane consumed the last of the food while he waited. It was several minutes before he was able to discern their presence when they finally emerged from the dark recesses of the engine room on the main deck.

"By the way, Captain," the skipper had begun, "there are a few rules I hold to. No one's ta be on the pilot house deck or in the boiler room 'cept my crew."

They started down the rampway toward the planking of the wharf. Masters paused to separate the papers in his hand as he spoke.

"Thet's reasonable ta be expected, 'n I'll see ta it." He offered a sheaf of papers to Kearney. "Here's yer set a my orders 'n official paperwork. I'll have my train here come an hour afta sunup."

"See ya then," the ship's skipper shook hands, then stuffed the papers in a side pocket of his coat. He waited on the slope of the ramp while the army officer tucked his papers in a breast pocket on his way toward his horse. Kearney's pipe had gone out some time ago. As he watched the other man's departure, he knocked the ashes from the bowl and slipped the cold pipe into the pocket with the papers.

Releasing the reins from the hitching post ring, Captain Masters mounted easily then turned his horse toward the shadowed streets which would take him from the town. As the horse's clatter faded and the Queen's captain turned from the wharf, Duane stepped hesitantly from the shadows.

"Captain Kearney, Sir," he called, unsure of the reception he might receive.

The captain stopped at the sound of the vaguely familiar voice and turned to observe the slight figure standing at the edge of the shadows.

"What is it, Boy? Don't I know you?" He screwed up his face in an attempt to see what he could not see in the dark of the night. "Come up here in the light so's I kin make ya out better."

Duane approached the man. It had been nearly four years since his pa had brought him to the big city and he wasn't sure the captain would know him. He certainly did not know the captain except by association with distant memories.

"I do know ya. But I can't say as it's been recent." He reached out as the boy approached and placed a calloused hand under the boy's chin to turn his face to a better light. "Why yer Andy Kinkade's boy, ain't ya?"

"Yes, Sir."

87

The same hand shifted to a shoulder to draw the boy toward the deck of the boat. "Come on aboard 'n tell me what brings ya lookin fer me."

"How'd ya know?" the boy asked as he walked with the man up the gangway.

"Ya wouldn't a asked fer me by name, fer one thin," the skipper began. He paused as they reached the deck of the Queen, and turned the boy to face him squarely. With both hands on the boy's shoulders and the deck lamplight on his own face, he continued. "Fer 'nother thin, ya wouldn't be here in the first place 'n ya wouldn't be packin a bedroll." There was a brief pause, but the boy looked him square in the face and the captain saw in those brown eyes a lonely determination and pain. "How are ya called?"

"I'm called Dee. My given name is Duane." He shifted his bedroll to ease the strain on his ribs.

"Ya wanna come up ta my cabin 'n tell me why yer here? It's a mite cold out 'n ya kin sit a spell while I've a cup a coffee."

"Okay."

Captain Kearney started toward a forward stairway. Duane followed at his side. As they mounted the steps, the pain from the day's travels rose once more in his consciousness and the boy was forced to stop and rest before continuing at a much slower pace.

"What's wrong with ya, Boy?" a concerned Kearney asked.

"Nothin, Sir."

"What da ya mean nothin?" the captain reached to relieve the boy of his gear. His hand was brushed aside. "It's plain ta see thet som'thin's hurtin ya. Now give me yer gear 'n ya kin say yer story when we're inside."

Reluctantly Duane allowed the man to take his burden for the remainder of the climb to the top deck. The two entered the warmth of the captain's quarters and closed the door against the winter chill. Duane's gear was parked on the floor near the door as Kearney offered him a chair on his way to the coffee pot on the stove.

"Take the chair at my desk, Dee. It's firm and should be good fer yer back." He poured a cup of coffee, then turned toward a large wooden rocker beside a small table.

"It's not my back, Sir," Duane returned as he settled into the swivel oak chair.

"Then tell me why yer here," he leaned back and sipped from the cup. "Why are ya painin so, Dee?"

"I need yer help, Captain." The boy rested his head against the back of the chair and closed his eyes a moment as he gave in to his exhaustion.

"Are ya okay, Son?" The boy nodded without comment. "Want somethin hot ta drink? There's hot cocoa in the galley."

"Yea," Duane acknowledged. "Thet sure would go good. I'm awful cold inside 'n tired."

"I'll be right back."

William Kearney set his cup on the table as he rose from the chair to cross the room to the door. "Ya kin look about while I'm out. Won't take long."

The boy opened his eyes at the sound of the door latch, took a deep breath, and rolled his head to the side to glance about the cabin. It was comfortably furnished and finished in fine woods. A small bookcase contained several leather-bound volumes, some finished in gilt trim. A painting on the wall depicted two sternwheelers belching smoke and cutting water in a river race. Some papers lay scattered on the writing surface of the open roll-top desk. The many pigeon holes were like little treasure troves with aging papers and a myriad of oddments. The door latch clicked as the man reentered carrying a small enameled teapot, steaming at the spout, and a tin cup. Somewhat rested, Duane sat up in the chair as the captain pushed the door shut, crossed to the desk, and poured the boy a cup of steaming cocoa. Duane sipped the refreshing warmth. Kearney heated the contents of his own cup before returning to the rocker.

"Better?" the man asked.

"Yea," the boy confirmed.

The captain held his cup with both hands just under his lips. "Tell me, Dee, why is't yer here."

There was a moment of quiet while Duane drained his cup, then set it on the desk. "Well, Sir," he began, "I'm lookin ta find my Pa. He left fer the war last spring. Last I heard from him, he was goin ta Fort Henry. But he ain't got my letters fer months. He don't know Ma's dead."

"What!" Kearney sat forward. "Yer ma's dead?"

"Kilt last summer by raiders."

"Thet how come ya be ta hurtin?"

"Yea. I was shot 'n left fer dead. Taday's ride in the wagon was pretty rough an made it hurt agin."

"What ride in the wagon? Tell ya what. Start ta the beginnin 'n I'll try ta sort this all out."

The two sat for another half hour while the boy's story unfolded and the man's many questions were answered, bringing into focus the reasons for and the nature of the quest that Duane was attempting to undertake.

"I'm not sure I agree with what yer wantin ta do, Dee." The man pulled at his chin thoughtfully. "I kin see why." He stood to refill his cup. "There's more cocoa in thet pot. Help yerself."

They drank in silence.

"Kin ya help me, Captain Kearney?" Duane finished the last of his beverage as he awaited a response.

The captain turned from the stove and crossed the room to his bunk against the wall. The boy swung the chair about to face him. "Tell ya what." The man leaned against the end rail. "Thet train ya came with is comin aboard at daylight on its way east. We'll be workin down rive' all the way ta Vicksburg. Thet's where they'll ketch the railroad fer wherever' they end up goin."

"How long's it take ta git there?"

"Depends on many thin's, like weather, currents, stops 'long the way. Reckon we should make it in five 'r six days. I'll take ya 'long 'n think on it durin the trip. If'n I decide so, I'll help ya git on yer way. But if not, ya come back up rive' with me 'n I see's ya git back ta Bendton. Ya gotta promise ya'll do as I think best.'

"I promise."

"Then 'tis settled. Ya'll put up in my cabin fer the trip. I'll git a spare bed from one a the passenger cabins tamorra. Ya'll use mine fer tanight."

Kearney moved to collect Duane's gear as the boy spoke. "Yes, Sir, but then they'll think I'm a sissy 'r thet I'm special 'r som'thin."

"Ya are special, Dee. I'm sure they'll understand if we explain the circumstances. Besides, whose ta give a dam. They don't even know ya rode with em." A sudden idea occurred to the captain and a sly smile creased at the corners of his mouth. "I jest put ya on as my cabin boy. Yer an official part a the crew. First thin come mornin, we'll fit ya up official lookin, uniform 'n all."

"Okay," the boy pushed to his feet. "Guess I'm awful tired."

The man separated the blankets from the food sack, untied the roll, and shook them open. Duane's extra clothing and a bundle of letters fell to the floor. They were scooped up and tossed onto a small wooden chair with the food sack, and the blankets were folded and laid at the foot of the bed.

"Throw yer clothes on thet same chair," the captain instructed as he turned down the bedcovers, "an climb in against the wall. There's plenty a room fer the two of us."

Duane crossed to the extra chair and stripped to his johns. As he removed his shirt, Kearney observed the scar on the side of his chest.

"How bad did they git ya?" he asked as he helped the boy up over the side of the wooden front.

"Couple a ribs 'n a piece a my head. But Pounder 'n me took two a them."

"Pounder?" he eased the boy to the back of the mattress as he pulled the covers up to his chin.

"My dog." Duane snuggled into a ball between the cold sheets.

"Yea. I fergot." He pushed the pillow under the boy's head. "I've several thin's ta tend ta fer I turn in. Ya sleep good now."

91

"Yes, Sir, Captain. Thanks."

William Kearney left the boy and crossed to his desk. Pulling the pipe and papers from his pocket, he put the pipe aside and spread the papers on the clutter of the writing surface. There he settled with a fresh cup of coffee to work with his papers. A half hour passed before he checked the fire in the stove, set aside his work, and considered turning in. Checking on the boy, he found him sleeping soundly with an arm hanging over the front edge of the bed and the covers kicked partway off. The man smiled affectionately as he pulled them back over the boy's shoulders. Lifting the blankets he had laid across the foot of the bunk, Captain Kearney turned down the lamp and settled in the wooden rocker for the night.

*　　*　　*

The grand commotion of a busy port reverberated in the early morning air. Bosses shouted orders. Winches creaked. Horses whinnied and hooves clattered on wooden planking. Men groaned under heavy loads. Crates grated against ramp and deck. Soldiers, deck hands, and dock workers were busy loading the wagons and other cargo, and leading horses to their temporary stabling. On board the Queen Captain Kearney supervised the placement of all that boarded his vessel. Captain Masters directed activity on the wharf.

Leaning over the railing of the top deck, Duane had a clear view of the activity below. He looked smartly dressed in the cabin boy uniform that Kearney had dug out of a wooden chest in the storage locker. Breakfast had been early, before the morning sun had begun to lighten the eastern sky. The boy had been introduced to some of his chores just after he was awakened when he was asked to clear pots and cups to the galley and return with fresh coffee. He also helped to set and clear the breakfast meal. The crew was on board at daybreak. Dock workers arrived shortly thereafter and began loading an assortment of cargo from the dock's clutter.

Captain Masters was as good as his word. The troop train arrived an hour after sunup and activity quickened to a fever pitch.

While the boy watched, teams were unhitched and led on board. Wagons were broken down as tongue and cross trees were removed from their brackets and loaded into the wagon beds. A dozen men bent their backs to the wheels and frames as they rolled them up the loading ramp and positioned them on the deck. Once spotted, wheels were blocked and ropes run through to secure them in their places. Some wagons had to be lifted on board by winch and derrick beam to be placed on the far side of the deck. Duane felt an excitement tingle from within as he watched the scene beneath him. He was surprised as he watched the soldiers about their work and realized many didn't have a regular uniform. Grey trousers were mixed with brown, blue, and black. They wore shirts of all colors and styles. Some had vests. Jackets, too, varied in style and color. Some were uniform, but many were not. He could smell the damp of the river, the hint of sweat and horses. Mingling, too, was the smell of wood smoke as the boilers were brought to pressure in readiness to set the paddle wheel into motion. Overhead was the whoosh of black smoke rolling from the stack. And somewhere was the hiss as surplus steam pressure escaped.

Activity subsided. The dock had been cleared of wagons and much of the assortment of freight. A new crowd had appeared as a score of young boys gathered to watch the activity of the departing steamboat. Footsteps approached on the forward stairsteps. Duane turned to see Captain Kearney appear from the lower deck, pipe in mouth, and a thin curl of smoke drifting behind his back.

"We goin now?" the boy asked.

"Shortly," the man replied as he took the pipe from his teeth. "Come on up ta the wheelhouse while we prepare ta cast off."

The boy followed the man up the last stairway to the wheelhouse deck. Once inside the glass-enclosed structure, Captain Kearney drew gently on the pipe as he approached the speaker tubes.

"Carney!" he hollered into a pipe.

"Aye, Captain?" a deep voice echoed back from below.

"Ya ready down there?"

"We're ready, Sir."

"Stand by. About five yet."

"Aye, Sir."

"Dee," he turned to the boy and pointed the pipe stem to a large flat table with long pigeon holes in series beneath. "See if thet's the chart a this part a the river."

"How kin I tell?' the boy asked, crossing to the table.

"Ya'll see the name Ozark in large letters near the center." While the boy checked the chart, the captain reached overhead and pulled the wooden grip on the whistle cord. A loud shrieking told all the Ozark Queen was about to cast off.

"Yes, Sir," Duane replied. "This says Ozark in the middle."

"Thanks," Kearney acknowledged as he stepped to the door.

The boy followed and watched from the doorway as the captain went to the rail to call to the deck hands and the Confederate captain.

"Captain Masters, are ya all secure down there?"

"Yes, Sir, Mr. Kearney," the officer replied from below.

"Linesmen, cast yer lines fore an aft. Keep them kids clear a the edge." He hurried back in and called on the speaking tube as he slipped the keeper ropes from the two sides of the wheel. "Carney, give me ahead slow."

"Aye, Sir," the voice replied.

Again the whistle shrieked as the vessel began to vibrate with a new sound and the drive beams pushed the great paddle wheel into motion. A movement caught the boy's eye as a young man in his early twenties moved to a small platform in the starboard railing in front of the pilot house. Duane became aware of a slow gliding movement as the captain turned the wheel and the town with its waterfront began to slip away. They were moving. Suddenly the boy's senses closed down. Everything was shut out as a muffled silence and an empty loneliness enveloped him and his immediate surroundings seemed to become strangely distant. The panic of his uncertain future passed as he sensed once more the aroma of the captain's pipe and could hear again the slow pulsing of the engine's machinery, the rush of the smoke from the twin stacks, and the creaking of the pilot wheel.

"Who's thet outside?" Duane asked.

"James Wyatt," Kearney replied. "He's watchin the river. Sometimes when we git ta tricky water we hafta measure an some'n will stand there an call the mark. He'll be in shortly. He's my cub pilot, learnin ta steer this craft. Once we're underway, he'll take the wheel."

Duane walked to a portside window where he looked back at the receding town as it dwindled into the distance. Warm sunlight flooded through the windows, glistening in the glass and sparkling off polished wood and brass fixtures.

"It seems quiet up here in a strange way," the boy observed.

"Now as we're on our way," the man suggested, "ya kin go on down 'n look about. I'll not be needin ya fer a hour 'r so."

"Okay," Duane agreed.

He walked out into bright sunlight, but was surprised by the chill of the moving air. Descending toward the main deck, he found the protection offered by the overhanging deck structure cut the draft and its chill. The lower decks were awash with activity as passengers strolled the upper deck and the soldiers lounged about on the cargo deck. Some stood to watch the passing shore line. Others settled on deck, cargo crates, against wagon wheel or cabin wall—to card game, a small conversation, or a tune on harmonica or guitar. A routine began to settle about the boat. Duane wandered through the small knots of soldiers until he found a spot he liked. Climbing onto a wagon seat, he settled to listen as a small group of soldiers shared their rendition of THE BONNIE BLUE FLAG.

A musically entertaining half hour drifted by before a card game exploded into angry words as a sore loser vented his anger.

"Come on, Sammy. Ya lost the hand fair 'n square an ya know it. Either shut up an play 'r go cool off." The voice bore the impatience of one tired of the same sore loser from previous experience.

"Yer all a pack a cheats!" The man jumped to his feet and threw a hand of cards in the face of the nearest soldier. He stormed away from the game and approached the group near Duane.

"Why don't ya shut up yer cat yowlin. Ya make a barnyard sound pretty." Insults fell of calloused listeners.

"Sergeant Winters," one suggested, "yer known ta be a sore loser. So go fer a walk 'n cool down."

As the angry figure turned to leave, his eyes fell on the boy perched on the wagon seat. "What's a snivlin brat like you sittin 'round in thet monkey suit fer?" His scowling voice grated and Duane cringed within. "Git down from there 'n git outta my sight. Else I jest might throw ya over the side." He moved menacingly toward the wagon.

One young red-head, fresh from the farm, stepped forward to confront the grizzled sergeant. "Ya best cool down, Sarg, 'er I'm gonna . . ."

"What!" the older man bellowed. "Yer way outta line, Soldier!" Before anyone realized what was happening, he reached up, grabbed Duane by the coat, and lifted him bodily from the wagon seat. The boy felt fear paralyze him from within and his desire to cry out remained silenced. "If I choose ta drop this monkey inta the river," he held the frightened boy up for all to see, "then I'll do it."

The red-head continued. "It might be I'm a farm boy, but I'm bigger 'n you. Ya best put thet boy down 'r I'll tear ya limb from limb!"

"Sergeant!" another voice challenged from the nearby stairs. "Ya harm a hair on my cabin boy 'n ya'll die right here on this river! Put him down!"

Duane felt himself lowered to firm footing on the boat's deck.

"Thanks," he barely whispered as the large hands released him.

"Mister!" Kearney continued, "I dunno what yer problem is, but this here boy's seen more hell then you have."

"No," Duane protested as the captain approached.

"They're gonna hear it, Dee," he placed a protective hand on the boy's shoulder as he stood beside him. "Ya've no shame." Nearby soldier's looked up to listen. "Dee's here on a search fer his pa. He's already been in combat with murderin raiders who kilt his ma an left him fer dead, too. He 'n his dog kilt two a them. Now he's done his piece a this war. Ya let him be. Save yer anger fer the enemy."

Silence. The sergeant jammed his hands into his pockets and walked away, his head bent low in shame. He passed from sight beyond the wagons. Kearney spoke quietly to the boy and they turned to climb the ladder toward the upper deck. The soldiers watched them go before exchanging surprised glances and entering into respectful talk about what they had just witnessed.

The day drifted on as the riverboat continued its journey downriver. Wild country and some scattered farmland extended as far as the eye could see along either side of the river. Late in the evening Duane descended from his supper chores to settle on the grand staircase at the front of the Queen and watch the gathering darkness of the eastern sky. Quiet conversation, music, and the soft strands of YELLOW ROSE drifted in the chill air to mingle with the throbbing of the boat's engines and the swoosh of billowing smoke and churning paddle.

A bearded figure approached from the port side and stopped to stand near the boy.

"Boy," he began with embarrassment. "Kin ya eve find it ta fergive me." He looked out toward the river. "I neve meant no harm. Sometimes I do bad thin's when I git mad at a person." He paused in awkward silence, then turned and his eyes met the boy's. They were dark with a hint of blue and a glistening of emotion. Duane knew he was sincere and his heart reached out to the man. The sergeant continued, "I ask ta be yer friend."

They searched each others eyes in silence and read into the depths of souls in pain. The boy smiled sadly. "My name's Dee. What's yers?"

"Sammy Winters, sergeant, Confederate Army."

"Hey, Sergeant Sammy Winters, I'm watchin the stars come. Ya wanna set here with me? I neve seen a river sky go ta night b'fer."

"Thet'd be good," the man responded.

He walked around to ascend the steps and settle on the broad tread beside the boy. They fell into a soft conversation, their voices lost in the mingled sounds of the evening. Night crept on, the velvet black reached out of the east and across the heavens, and a broken moon joined a million bits of light to cast a ghostly glow on a ribbon of river, the two figures seated on the grand staircase, and the vessel journeying onward in the night.

*   *   *

In the days that followed, Duane spent all his spare time mingling with the company of soldiers on the cargo deck. His story was quickly known to them and they accepted him with respect. There were a few who withheld their friendship, but most enjoyed his presence. Sergeant Winters became his unofficial guardian and was mellowed through his companionship with the boy. He watched for Duane to arrive on deck and was inseparable until Duane departed to undertake the duties of his position. There was little to do but talk, play cards, or share song and music; except when it came one's turn to clean the temporary stables, feed the horses, or help with meal preparations.

The boredom of routine was broken late on the second day when the Queen approached the small port at Pine Bluff. The shrill cry of the boat's whistle pierced the afternoon air to alert the populace of her coming. Duane watched with the sergeant at his side. The boy was perched on a wagon wheel for a better view; the man leaned against the corner of the wagon's bed. It had been an unusually warm day. Their clothing was clammy from perspiration so they had unbuttoned their shirts, pulled out the tails, and folded up their sleeves.

As the boat neared the wharf, boys swimming in the river stopped to watch. How refreshing the water must feel, Duane thought as he watched. Some climbed a tree on the shoreline to wave and shout to the boat's crew. Others swam out to meet her. On board the Ozark Queen, the deck was chaotic with commotion as the crew prepared to dock. Some of the crew stood by to throw mooring lines to shore hands standing ready on the wharf. Others prepared to run out the gangplank. As naked swimmers approached the vessel, some of the soldiers and the deck hands reached to haul them from the water. An air of enthusiastic excitement grew in the movement of the boys scrambling on board and the preparations for docking. The lively chatter of bragging rights from the first to reach the deck and all who dared to take the challenge mixed with the shouting of orders, the heartbeat of the engine room, the whinnies of startled horses, shouted conversations, and the rush of water rolling from under the vessel's bow. Some of the new arrivals sat on the edge of the deck with their feet dangling in the rough splash of the wake. Others visited with members of the crew known from previous stops or stood poised to return to the river as the boat neared the wharf, or hung in the water clinging to the edge of the shallow hull.

Captain Kearney's orders rang from overhead. "Ya deckhands git them boys on deck ta haul their feet in 'n them in the water ta swim clear. We're comin in now!"

Duane watched as those in the water shoved off to swim clear and head for the shallows beyond the wharf. But one toe-headed ten-year-old slipped as he tried to push off.

"Sammy!" Duane pointed to the water, "thet boy's in trouble!"

"Hold on!" Winters called. "I'll haul ya out!"

A look of helpless horror froze on the youngster's face as he slipped along the boat's hull toward the stern and the menacing motion of the paddle wheel.

The sergeant hurried along the edge of the deck, trying frantically to catch up to the figure in the water. Duane jumped down from his perch on the wagon wheel and dashed toward the engine room.

"Carney! Stop the wheel!" he screamed in panic. "A kid's caught in the water!"

The noise of the pistons driving the rockers and beams which powered the wheel, thundered about him as he entered the dark cavity of machinery. The engineer could not hear the boy, but sensed the urgency of his actions. Dumping the steam pressure with an explosive hissing, Carney threw the reverse lever and returned steam to ease the moving beams to a stop. The returning pressure had to be increased slowly or the machinery would be damaged and the large paddles broken. Even as Carney worked to stop the turning wheel, Duane dashed outside to see if Winters had caught the boy.

At first no one realized what was happening. The sudden slowing of the great wheel brought about the stunning realization of the crisis which was unfolding. Duane dashed between wagons and swung around the wheel rim to sprint toward the back edge of the deck. He saw as Sammy neared the struggling boy and jumped from the deck's edge to land in the water with hand outstretched toward the child.

The man went under on impact, but managed to clasp the boy's wrist and hang on. As he bobbed to the surface, the two drifted against the Queen's side, pulled by her momentum toward the moving wheel. The sergeant pulled the boy close and hooked his arm around the naked waist, at the same time guiding their roll in the water's current to slide toward the rotating paddles feet first.

Duane ran to the end of the deck where the stern overhung the water beside the giant wheel. There was nothing he could do but watch. He felt alone and helpless, completely unaware that all aboard the Queen and along the dock had become witness to the unfolding drama. But the sergeant was in control. He planted his shoes against the edge of the paddle and pushed away as it slowly dipped into the water. It wasn't enough to break clear, but the slackened speed of the engine allowed time to prepare for the impact of the next paddle. Duane saw Winters say something to the boy, then hug him close against his chest as the broad paddle struck him from behind pushing both beneath the murky waters. A hush fell on the scene. A moment later the two bobbed to the surface in the foamy wash behind the vessel.

Loud cheers erupted when the boy and the man waved toward the boat and began their swim toward shore. Duane stood on the small piece of stern deck, holding the brace beam to the wheel for balance. Silent tears slid down his cheeks as he cried quietly, relieved that a tragedy had been avoided.

The Ozark Queen slid softly into place beside the wharf. Once more the air hummed with activity as the boy turned to walk toward the gangplank, leave the boat, and seek out his friend and the boy he had saved.

Captain Kearney paused in his descent from the pilot house deck to stand at the rail and watch as his cabin boy disappeared in the rush of activity on the wharf. Carney had reported on the speaking tube what had happened in the engine room. There goes one special boy, the man thought to himself. It was time to have a talk with Captain Masters. He would attend to that once they were underway. For now, there was work to do.

*　*　*

Early the following morning the steamboat set out to continue its journey southeast. A company of fifty-odd soldiers had joined the ship's roster along with a shipment of military stores. Included with rifles and munitions was a small collection of band instruments. The newly arrived soldiers had with them several musicians. As life aboard the Ozark Queen returned to its routine of monotony, some relief was to be enjoyed as musicians from both companies combined their talents and interests to render several spontaneous concerts.

On the second day out from Pine Bluff, the weather turned to a grey drizzle. The men huddled about in parkas and coats, as far back under the overhead deck as possible. Even so, the wind-driven mist soaked their clothing and dripped from soggy hat brims. In the warmth of the pilot house, Duane enjoyed a good view of the river through droplet-coated glass, alive with squiggly chasings as moisture gathered enough weight to dash downward toward the sills. The river was broad at this point with a wide safe channel. The shorelines were often settled with farmlands and small towns. Under normal circumstances, the Queen would be making many stops each day. But this trip she carried men and munitions for the army and both required quick passage.

Captain Kearney called the boy's attention to the town of Napoleon along the shoreline to the south and to changing forces of river current evident in the rippling of the water's surface, and evident, too, in changes of the water's color and texture. Here the Arkansas River joined the great Mississippi. Slowly, as the riverboat entered upon the great waterway, moving further out from the shoreline, it became lost in the loneliness of water and drizzle.

In the ghostly greyness, the captain sounded the steamboat's whistle. It cut sharply through the thick weather, warning other vessels of the Queen's presence. Other whistles announced other vessels passing unseen. By late afternoon the weather was clear and the bustling traffic of the river highway was a sharp contrast to the lonely passage along the Arkansas.

As large as the Mississippi was, it twisted, backtracked, sidestepped, and turned so erratically that the journey was slower and of a more hazardous nature. The river was always changing, Kearney explained. New bends, islands, sand bars, and channels came and were lost from one trip to the next. Vicksburg was about a hundred miles south of Napoleon. But the river's wanderings nearly doubled the distance.

The last day dawned crisp and brilliant. In the early afternoon, Jamie Wyatt was at the wheel. Captain Kearney leaned over the chart table with Duane and pointed out their location on the map.

"We're comin round the point, now, Sir," Jamie announced. He spun the wheel hard to starboard and the Queen began a wide turn from a northeast heading, full-about to a heading of southwest.

Looking up at his pilot's comment, the captain pointed the stem of his pipe toward the distant shore outside the starboard window. "See off there ta the south?" he spoke.

Duane followed the outstretched arm, peering beyond the wisp of tobacco smoke to a series of land points barely visible in the afternoon sun.

"I think I see more channels," the boy stated "There's so many. How da ya know which way ta go?"

"It takes knowin the rive' real good. Thet's why ya start as a cub pilot an learn ta read the water 'n know the rive' fer ya eve' pilot yer own boat." Still pointing, the man explained the current landmark. "The clearin furthest ta right marks the side a the main channel. Thet's Milliken's Bend. Beyond there it's only one more set a bends round the mouth a the Yazoo River b'fer Vicksburg."

The boy watched the approaching landmark. For a few minutes nothing more was said. The vessel swung easily through the last arc of her turn until she was in line to follow the main channel. Milliken's Bend drifted off the starboard side, then slipped gently behind.

"Come on, Dee," Kearney instructed. "We've some thin's ta tend ta fer we reach port." He started toward the door. "Mr. Wyatt, ya hold yer course. I'll be back in a half hour."

"Yes, Sir, Mr. Kearney."

The boy followed the captain through to the deck.

"Ya go ta the main deck 'n bring Captain Masters ta my cabin," Kearney spoke as they reached the ladder. "I'll meet ya there."

Duane passed through the commotion of activity on the lower decks, passed the skipper's order to Captain Masters by way of Sergeant Reilly, and tarried to visit with Sammy Winters while the sergeant searched for the officer.

"Dee," Captain Masters called as he worked his way through the clutter of humanity lounging about the sun-shadowed deck, "Sergeant Reilly tells me yer lookin fer me."

"Yes, Sir. Captain Kearney wants ta see ya in his cabin." He spoke once more to Sergeant Winters before the captain arrived. "Soon's I kin, I'll be back down."

"I'll be here," the sergeant acknowledged. "Ya run 'long now."

Following protocol which Captain Kearney had begun to teach the cabin boy, Duane led and the captain followed. "This way, Sir." They ascended to the quarters on the upper deck. There Duane opened the door and announced the captain.

"Come in, both a ya," Kearney invited. "Dee, fergit the formalities 'n bring yerself a chair. Captain, take the rocker."

As the two made themselves comfortable, Kearney settled into the chair at his desk and drew quietly on his pipe while he awaited their attention.

"Dee," he began, "when we started this trip tagether I said I'd think on yer askin me fer help. An I've done a heap a thinkin. Captain," he paused to exhale a light cloud of aroma and to collect his thoughts, "yer familiar with the boy's story?"

"I've heard it," he glanced at Duane.

"Da ya know why he's on this boat?"

"I assumed he was workin fer ya."

"No Sir. He come ta me ta help him git ta the war so's he kin find his pa. I've bin givin it thought all 'long the way 'n I have a idea if yer willin ta help, too."

The boy sat forward with elbows on knees and chin on clasped hands, listening intently as the discussion unfolded. Kearney sucked gently on his pipe while the officer responded.

"How kin I help?" he asked.

There was a brief pause to lay the pipe aside and release a small cloud of tobacco smoke. It hung briefly in the air as it faded to a wisp of pleasant odor.

"Yer company's on its way fer assignment ta the army up north near Tennessee. We figure Dee's pa ta be up thet way. Ain't it so, Dee?"

"Yes, Sir," Duane confirmed. "His last letter says he's goin ta help git Grant at Fort Henry."

"We lost Fort Henry last month," Masters informed. "Ain't ya heard? Grant took Henry 'n Donelson, too."

The news came as a stunning blow. The boy was suddenly drained of all enthusiasm. It didn't matter any more. There was no reason left to go on. He cried within, but the tears did not come. A blank stare passed beyond the wall in front, focusing on nothingness.

"Dee," the captain continued, "thet don't mean yer pa's lost. A lot a our troops slipped away fer the end an only the garrison was taken prisoner. Even so, there's talk of a prisoner exchange."

Duane cheered up and listened while Captain Kearney continued. "Thet all bein what it is, I figger the captain's comp'ny could use a drummer boy 'n Dee here could go on with ya. When ya hitch up with the big army, ya could look up his pa 'n he could think on what ta do next."

There was a short silence while all three considered the skipper's proposal.

"Would thet help ya, Dee?" the officer inquired.

"Yes, Sir!" the boy beamed, breaking into a smile.

"We kin do it," Captain Masters agreed. "We'll check with our quartermaster 'n fit ya up with a uniform an see if the musicians from the Pine Bluff company have an extra drum. I'll have my lieutenant add ya ta the company roster. By the time we're arrived ta Vicksburg ya'll be an official drummer boy. Maybe we'll even find one who kin learn ya how ta play."

"Yer set, Dee," Kearney stated. "We'll git yer gear packed 'n see if yer sergeant friend kin find ya a have'sack fer ta put it in." He stood and extended his hand to the officer. "Captain, we sure thank ya fer yer help."

Masters rose from the rocker as the boy, too, stood. "Glad I could." He accepted the outstretched hand. "We best git ta puttin this in order. It won't be much longer." He turned to the boy. "Dee, ya come with me 'n we'll git ya outfitted. Then ya come back 'n pack yer thin's."

The three started for the door as the captain finished. "Captain, I'll see ta the boy's needs at present 'n see ya later fer we go ashore."

"Thet'll be fine. I'll be busy fer a time until we tie up."

They left the cabin. The boy and the officer departed below. The skipper paused to watch them go and to knock the ashes from his pipe, then turned to climb back to the pilot house.

The Queen passed the mouth of the Yazoo and rounded the point to a heading northeast. Within the half hour the river rounded the point of land to the right, revealing high bluffs on the far bank and the city perched on its top.

During this time Captain Masters and Sergeant Winters had worked to transform Duane from a cabin boy to a drummer boy, and to equip him for his new lifestyle in the army. It wasn't much for a uniform. He wore his own trousers with an oversized brown shirt and grey forage cap. Now the captain was busy with the many details in preparation of landfall. Duane stood near the bow of the main deck, his arm around a deck support post against which he rested his weight. Sammy stood at his side with a protective arm across the boy's shoulders. They gazed in awe at the great city atop the bluffs—the biggest place either had seen in his lifetime. The river ahead was alive with motion. The great wharf had several riverboats at its side.

As the boat's whistle echoed off the surrounding hills, the boy thought back over the events of the past two weeks. Home seemed so far away and so long ago. He missed Jamie, Mrs. Riggs, his ma, his home. God, how lonely he felt! A sharpness stung in his eyes and throat. His vision blurred as tears slipped quietly down his cheeks. Sergeant Winters sensed the boy's lonesome grief and squeezed the small shoulder gently to say he cared. Duane slipped both arms around the strong waist and buried his face in the folds of the man's shirt. He cried quietly as Sammy held him close. Momentarily the boy pulled away and wiped his face with the back of the sleeve on his new shirt.

"I'm okay," he announced.

"Thet's good," Winters acknowledged. "Cause we've a whole lot a work ta do ta git unloaded and move in ta the army camps. Here tell we won't stay here long, though. They got a railroad thet'll take us north in no time."

"I neve seen a railroad b'fer. But I heard of it," the boy stated.

"I ain't seen one either," the sergeant added. "Guess it's a first time fer both of us."

Deckhands moved about to prepare the mooring lines, the gangplanks, derricks, and winch lines. Captain Masters called his subordinates together to assign work details for unloading wagons and horses and for reassembling wagon parts and harnessing up the teams.

"Where da we go from here?" Duane asked as the sergeant turned to go to the captain.

"As I hear it, the army's gatherin up north at a place called Corinth. The railroads go through there from all parts." He was gone toward the meeting which was held at the first wagon.

Commotion crescendoed about the boat. Passengers gathered at the upper rail. Soldiers from both companies set to work to free wagons and cargo from safety lines which had held them in place. The engines changed their rhythmic pounding as the vessel slowed for docking. The whistle shrieked. Foremen shouted orders. Duane found himself drawn in on a work detail preparing one of the wagons to be rolled down the rampway to the wharf. The din of noise closed in about him as the Ozark Queen slipped between two other riverboats and bumped gently against the timbers of the dock.

This was Vicksburg. It was the end of the trip. It was the beginning of a new journey.

Behind lay the boy's childhood.

Ahead lay war.

About the author, J. Arthur Moore

J. Arthur Moore is an educator with 42 years experience in public, private, and independent settings. He is also an amateur photographer and has illustrated his works with his own photographs. In addition to *Journey into Darkness*, Mr. Moore has written *Summer of Two Worlds*, "Heir to Balmawr", a drama for his fifth grade students, a number of short pieces, and short stories. His latest work is a short story titled "West to Freedom."

A graduate of Jenkintown High School, just outside of Philadelphia, Pennsylvania, he attended West Chester State College, currently West Chester University. Upon graduation, he joined the Navy and was stationed in Norfolk, Virginia, where he met his wife to be, a widow with four children. Once discharged from the service, he moved to Coatesville, Pennsylvania, began his teaching career, married and brought his new family to live in a 300-year-old farm house in which the children grew up and married, went their own ways, raised their families to become grandparents themselves.

Retiring after a 42-year career, Mr. Moore has moved to the farming country in Lancaster County, Pennsylvania, where he plans to enjoy the generations of family and time with his model railroad, and time to guide his writings into a new life through publication. It also allows time for traveling to Civil War events, presenting at various organizations and events, time with adopted grandchildren (five former students who were key to the 6-month move project and have become family), and, having saved the camp equipment from years of programs with schools and in the summer, the chance to build a camp site in the back yard for the kids.

Edwards Brothers Malloy
Thorofare, NJ USA
September 3, 2013